D0938112

Merab's Beauty
and Other Stories

ALSO BY TORGNY LINDGREN

Bathsheba (novel)

Merab's Beauty

and Other Stories

Including "The Way of a Serpent"

TORGNY LINDGREN

Translated from the Swedish by
Mary Sandbach and Tom Geddes

MECHANICS' INSTITUTE

1817

HARPER & ROW, PUBLISHERS, New York
Grand Rapids, Philadelphia, St. Louis, San Francisco
London, Singapore, Sydney, Tokyo, Toronto

Merab's Beauty was first published in Sweden under the title *Merabs skönhet,* 1983.

Legender was first published in Sweden, 1986.

The Way of a Serpent was first published in Sweden under the title *Ormens väg på hälleberget,* 1982.

All three titles were published by P. A. Norstedt & Söners Förlag, Stockholm.

Merab's Beauty © 1983 by Torgny Lindgren
Legender © 1986 by Torgny Lindgren
The Way of a Serpent © 1982 by Torgny Lindgren
Translation © 1989 by William Collins Sons & Co., Ltd.

FIRST EDITION

Designed by Alma Orenstein

Library of Congress Cataloging-in-Publication Data
Lindgren, Torgny, 1938–
    [Short stories. English. Selections]
    Merab's beauty and other stories / Torgny Lindgren; translated from the Swedish by Mary Sandbach and Tom Geddes.—1st ed.
    p. cm.
    ISBN 0-06-016229-5
    1. Lindgren, Torgny, 1938– —Translations, English. I. Title.
PT9876.22.I445A27 1990
839.7'374—dc20   89-33221

---

90 91 92 93 **94** CC/HC 10 9 8 7 6 5 4 3 2 1

Contents

vii

The publishers gratefully acknowledge the contribution made by The Swedish Institute toward the cost of this English translation.

Merab's Beauty

Translated by
Mary Sandbach

Tailor Molin

MOLIN had learned tailoring in Jörn. But what he made was no good.

An overcoat for Nylundius the preacher, the man who pretty certainly was the father of Isabella Stenlund's illegitimate boy; the coat was far too small in the waist and horribly broad across the shoulders. It was impossible to preach in it. And a coat for Sabina of Avabäck, but it was so tight that Sabina couldn't button it up. And the black suit for Konrad Israelsson of Lakaberg: it was so badly cut that he could wear it only in church, for there it couldn't be seen.

After that there was no one who would have anything made by Molin.

The Molins had moved into Sara Lundmark's house, the little house this side of Inreliden, after she was dead. It was Jacob Lundmark's Gerda who had charge of the place. She thought it would be a good thing to have someone looking after the house.

"It's pride," said Tailor Molin. "They've always been proud in these parts. And poverty. They haven't the money for tailor-made clothes."

His woman, Judith, was large and handsome, her hair was black and wavy and she looked as if she had painted around her eyes, though in fact she had not; she had dimples and she often laughed to show her splendid teeth. No one could explain how he had got hold of her, how he had conquered her, for he was a poor thing. He had a hump. Not a big hump, but all the same.

And people said: "With his sharp little needle in that seam of hers."

But they were childless. And people said: "He sews crookedly and his needle is too weak."

He bought dungaree cloth from Umeå and made overalls, both tops and trousers, and he sold them at Lycksele market. And he said: "Folly is exalted while excellent men are degraded."

He had wanted to make tailcoats, morning coats, and frock coats, not overalls.

But just the same it brought him in a few crowns.

All his life he went on making overalls, and today you can still find overall tops sewn by him.

Even after he did well with his wall hangings he sewed overalls now and then.

But it was like this with the wall hangings.

One evening he made a hanging of bits and pieces; there was corduroy, blue serge, dungaree cloth, and denim, he made a wall hanging and also a frame to go around it made of moleskin and he put two rings on it to hang it up by. He sewed his hanging only to gladden his heart and because he had nothing else to do. And in the middle of the hanging it said in blue letters:

REJOICE WITH TREMBLING

Anton Lundmark from Lakaberg came and caught sight of the hanging. He had really come to get a new lining for his dog-skin fur coat; he had three homesteads up at Malå which he was obliged to visit in the winter and then he needed a dog-skin fur coat. He had two: this was his old one, and then he caught sight of the hanging and so he said: "I can give you two crowns for that hanging."

And that wasn't a bad offer. But Tailor Molin hesitated all the same.

"If you order a suit then you can have the hanging as well," he said.

"I have suits," said Anton Lundmark. "And clothes are only for outward show. But that hanging now, it's about the soul and eternity."

On no account was he going to say that he didn't want a badly made suit, he wanted to be finely, inoffensively, and piously dressed. He had his suits made in Norsjö, he could afford it and he was a juryman; the clothes he wore had to display power and dignity.

"I only took those words out of the psalms," said Tailor Molin.

"I know," said Anton Lundmark. "But you have made them great, and sewn them so that they can be hung up on a wall. Words can always be found, but they first come alive when you say them or spell them or hang them up on a wall."

That testimony from Anton Lundmark stuck fast in Tailor Molin's mind. He never forgot it, he knew it word for word as long as he lived; almost everything he heard he was able to repeat word for word as long as he lived, and he lived right up to 1947. During his last years he was blind, then he sewed only with his fingers.

And two crowns was money all the same.

And his wall hangings were beautified and decked out with symbols and pictures of which Tailor Molin alone knew the meaning.

Later, when Anton Lundmark had gone, Tailor Molin said to Judith: "Words have raised up the man who stumbled and to faltering knees they have given strength. I may as well put together another couple of hangings."

And he sewed two hangings that very evening: HOME SWEET HOME MY SAFETY'S SHIELD and CHARITY NEVER FAILETH.

It was Gerda Lundmark, Jacob's Gerda, and Evald Sundström from Mörken who bought these hangings: Evald had a brother to whom he intended to give the hanging, that was the hanging about Charity; they were deadly enemies, those brothers.

And people came to ask if he had not more hangings, and many knew themselves what was to be put on them, and that was words from the Bible and old proverbs and thoughts that had been passed down.

And Tailor Molin accepted the orders and to Judith he said: "Clothes are a worldly matter. But words are the bread of life." However many he made, they were all sold.

And even Konrad came wanting two hangings. On one it said:

KONRAD ISRAELSSON

and on the other:

KONRAD FROM LAKABERG

And one he was going to put up in the kitchen and the other in the parlor.

But after a time, after some months, all the houses round about had wall hangings, and no more were needed.

Then Judith said: "If you sew them I will sell them."

And that's what they did. Though Tailor Molin said: "But you should not need to."

"You know well enough, Molin," she said, "that I am quite able to walk to the end of the earth."

He sewed, they were the same words he had sewn for the folk in Mörken and Inreliden and Kullmyrliden and Lakaberg and Sikträsk, but he made most of them with MY HOME MY JOY AND HAPPINESS and IN MY DISTRESS I CRIED UNTO THE LORD and Judith rolled them up and put them into the birchbark basket she carried on her back and went around selling them.

And Tailor Molin's wall hangings were also a success in Risliden and Björkås and Kallisberg and Bjunsele and Nyberg and Avaliden and Manjaur and Rålund, yes even in Norsjö itself.

But in Finnträsk there was a man called Holmberg, Otto Holmberg.

He was a widower and kept the smithy. He was large and fat and had a full beard. He played the accordion. He kept sheep. It was there Judith stayed, there with him.

It was like this.

She knew how to make cheese from sheep's milk, and she promised to teach him how to do it. He had bought a hanging; he would fetch the rennet she needed from Avaberg. It was the following night before he came back. The rennet had to lie for twelve hours in salt water, so she was obliged to stay until the next day.

Before they went to bed he played the accordion for her.

And when night came he wanted to lie with her, it was in the kitchen. She had made a bed for herself on the kitchen settle.

"Don't violate me," she said. "Don't do anything so mad."

"You are too good for Tailor Molin," he said. "You need a real man. A man like an Ardennes stallion."

"Where should I go with my shame?" she said.

"I haven't got a hump," said Otto Holmberg. "Feel up my back, it's like a barn door."

"Tailor Molin's hump is so small," she said. "I never think about that little hump."

"I've lain alone for three years," he said. "It's like perishing from thirst."

"It is Tuesday today," she said. "Tailor Molin is waiting for me, before the weekend I must be back in Inreliden."

"It's impossible for a man alone to keep himself warm. Solitude is like frost and like frozen ground."

"I won't do it," she said. "I'm not a loose liver; because I go about selling hangings I'm not bad."

But he did not listen to her. "A single log does not burn," he said. He grew wild and furious and his hands were like pincers; she could not defend herself.

And after she had made the sheep's-milk cheese the next morning she stayed there. She could not bring herself to go home to Tailor Molin and say: "Otto Holmberg in Finnträsk has lain with me; he was like a wild animal. I was only going to make sheep's-milk cheese for him. He played the accordion for me. He was like a ravenous wolf. He quite lost his head."

And she said to Otto Holmberg, "Now I am a lost woman."

And so she stayed there. She was there for four years, and people said to her: "But you are married to Tailor Molin."

"Yes," she said. "And I can never give him up."

It was Anton Lundmark who went and told Tailor Molin; he did it out of Christian love. He thought that Tailor Molin had a right to know what most people knew already.

"So she's left you," he said, "and moved in with that Otto Holmberg in Finnträsk."

That was on Saturday. He'd thought she would come home that evening. She'd said: "At the latest on Saturday. When the basket is empty I shall come home. At the latest on Saturday evening."

8

And afterward people asked Anton Lundmark: "But what did he say when you told him about it?"

"He said nothing. But he seemed to get the shivers. And he cut his hand with his razor blade. He was holding his razor blade to rip up cloth."

"So he was sitting sewing? A wall hanging?"

"Yes, he had sewn HE REMAINETH DEAD WHO but he had stopped there and I bandaged his hand. 'You mustn't bleed to death for her sake,' I said. 'She's wonderfully handsome, but she is not worth your sacrificing your life.' And I made him a cup of coffee, for he was, as it were, helpless.

"And I said to him: 'That's the way of adulteresses: they enjoy themselves to the full and then they wipe their mouths.' "

"But he said nothing?"

"No, he was as quiet as a lamb is with the man who shears it, and I had to help him into bed, for he seemed to be paralyzed. But it was clean and well made there in his bed, so dirty she isn't; however, even if he now manages, I shall send Eva there with a bit of bread and pickled pork."

But on Monday he sat sewing again. He was finishing that hanging, there was only DOTH NOT LOVE that was missing, and after that he did nothing for two weeks but sew hangings, and when Eva, Anton Lundmark's Eva, came with pickled pork and a bit of bread and a couple of liters of skimmed milk, he had a whole pile of hangings by his feet. And he told her he did not lack for anything, he had bought cheese and hard bread and pork in Kullmyrliden; as yet he was not any sort of pauper, he did not want alms, she could take the food back to Anton. And Eva, she did not gainsay him. She'd learned from Anton Lundmark never to contradict. She was quiet and meek. Anton Lundmark was her head. She was pale and rather thin; she had some sort of heart trouble. But she did not dare to take home those bits of food. Anton Lundmark was an upright man but he hated ingratitude. He loved his neighbor but he wanted him to be respectful, so Eva was obliged to bury the pork and bread in the heap of manure by the summer barn.

After that Tailor Molin went himself to sell his wall hangings, and people learned how things were: they knew that Judith had deserted him, that she lived with that Otto Holmberg in Finnträsk, so they bought from him, to be some sort of comfort to him in his misery, even those who had already bought hangings to give him a bit of happiness.

But compassion is not long-lasting, it devours itself, so he was later forced to hit on something else.

That was how it came about that he began to tell his stories, that's the explanation. And his stories, they still exist, they are like his wall hangings and his overall tops.

First he was given a cup of coffee and a bit of bread, then he reeled off a story; and he chose carefully between them—it would not do to talk about just anything to anyone—and then he could sell a hanging.

And people said: "They are darker than they used to be, those hangings of yours."

"That depends on the cloth," he said.

For the most part they were stories that people had already heard, they always knew the end, but they wanted to hear the words. The words were unusual: the events were not remarkable. And the people he told stories about were all of them old acquaintances. A story is only a picture, said Tailor Molin, and he even told stories about people who were still alive, but that didn't matter for it was the truth—the sum of many words is always in some way the truth.

And they said: "He's like a book of chronicles."

And people who did not want to have a hanging, they didn't offer coffee and they never asked: "How did things go in this place or that and for this man or that woman, you who know everything?"

He knew the words by heart, at least that's what he said—sermons he'd heard, letters that he'd been allowed to read, and stories he'd heard from others and those he himself had told sometime in the far past.

If you count the first year when he was brushing up his memory and the last three years when he only went out for two weeks in the year, it added up to thirty-eight years of wall hangings, storytelling, and now and then overalls.

But he never went to Finnträsk, he was afraid of meeting Judith.

Then Eva Lundmark, Anton's Eva, died, it was her heart.

By then Judith had lived in Finnträsk for four years. She was just as handsome as before, and her sheep's-milk cheese was even sold in a shop in Skellefteå.

Then Anton Lundmark went to Finnträsk; he knew that Otto Holmberg had gone to Lycksele to sell sheepskin rugs. It was in March and he had his boat-shaped sleigh and on the horse his hoops of bells.

"How long will you live in sin like this?" he said to Judith.

She said nothing. But she set out cheese and coffee; you can put sheep's-milk cheese in coffee and eat it with a spoon.

"He who sins, he is of the devil," said Anton Lundmark.

And what could she say?

"The chaff will be burned up with unquenchable fire."

Yes, that was how it was.

"Those who live in sin shall pass away to eternal punishment, but the righteous to eternal life."

And she was obliged to hold her tongue and agree: the righteous shall pass on to eternal life.

"And now I need a housekeeper. Someone to look after the house, who can cook. Eva had heart trouble, and was bidden home; she was recalled. It's bland and good this sheep's-milk cheese, and I have a maidservant, so it's to be a housekeeper."

"Yes," said Judith, "that's understood."

"Someone must take pity on you, Judith, and deliver you from sin," said Anton Lundmark.

She filled his cup of coffee.

"Tailor Molin goes around telling his stories," he said. "Stories he knows by heart. And sells wall hangings."

And then Judith said: "No one has his gifts. He is like a revelation."

And then all was quiet for a while.

She was not forty and Anton was the better part of sixty. Before they left she fed the sheep so that they would be all right for two days, and she took with her a sheepskin rug that Otto Holmberg had promised her. She had the rug over her in the sleigh and on top she had her basket. And Anton said: "I shall pay you with money, not with sheepskins."

And the whole way to Lakaberg he whistled. "Whither shall I then flee from the deep mire of sin?"

When they got back Judith said: "You have not understood this. No, Anton Lundmark, you have not understood this."

Even on that first night he was obliged to lie with her. Eva had been weak for a long time and lamentable and useless, and now he was a widower, and in the first place it was his soul that needed comfort—charity never faileth, charity forgiveth all, God looks with pleasure on love, and in true love there is no sin.

And when Tailor Molin got to know that now she had moved to Lakaberg, that now she was living with Anton Lundmark and was called his housekeeper, this is what he said: "It is twenty kilometers to Finnträsk and only six to Lakaberg, now at least she is on her way home."

But he did not go to Lakaberg, he went far out of his way

in order not to come near Lakaberg. AVOID THAT WHICH MAY ANGER YOU.

Otherwise he never mentioned Judith and no one spoke to him about her, her name never needed to cross his lips. And people knew how it was, he had her inside his thoughts, he could not bring himself to speak of her.

All the same he seemed to be managing; in the winter he sewed and in the summer he traveled, and he never needed help, though of course he was as thin as always.

In the spring when Judith had been two years in Lakaberg, Tailor Molin sewed a special wall hanging for Otto Holmberg in Finnträsk. He had thought about the words for a long time.

And he went for one purpose: he went as far as Finnträsk just because of that hanging.

They recognized one another, so nothing much was said.

When Tailor Molin had sat there for a good while and they had studied each other both long and well, then he said: "I have made a hanging for you, Otto."

Otto Holmberg said nothing.

"This hanging," said Tailor Molin. "Over the years this hanging has become something I have very much at heart."

And that wasn't anything for Otto Holmberg to say anything about.

"Nowadays I only sew the words I have in my heart."

And Otto Holmberg looked at the hanging, it was rolled up and Tailor Molin was sitting twisting it around and around between his hands, it was as if he did not really know whether or not to let Otto Holmberg read the words.

"Sewn words are long-lived," he said. "You can never know if they will ever be lost."

But in the end he unrolled the hanging and held it out to Otto Holmberg. He stretched it out in front of himself with straight arms, and the hanging had dark red borders:

HE WHO STEALS A HUMAN BEING
SHALL BE PUNISHED WITH DEATH

And Otto Holmberg looked at the hanging. Then he took two steps, the distance between them was no greater, and he seized hold of the hanging. He took hold of it by the top and wrenched it from Tailor Molin's hands and tore it to pieces as if it had been paper; the cloth rustled and screamed as it was rent between his fingers, and he threw the scraps onto the floor and stamped on them. Not a single letter was left in one piece; his hands were like a shredding machine. And when he had finished with the hanging he set to work on Tailor Molin. It was as if he wanted to treat him in the same way as the hanging. He took hold of his shoulders and wrenched and shook him as if he wanted to tear him in two pieces, and Tailor Molin's head hit the wall behind him, and the corner of the table thrust into his ribs, and his knees were banged on the floor time after time, and it hurt so much that he would have screamed aloud if it had not been that he saw that Otto Holmberg was in pain too; he was in such pain that he was weeping. They knew both of them how horribly hard it was to live without Judith, and Tailor Molin knew that all the same the words he had sewn were the right ones. In the midst of his agony he somehow felt content.

And when Otto Holmberg couldn't manage to tear and pull and shake anymore, he picked up Tailor Molin with one hand as if he had been a baby, opened the door, and flung him out, and all the time he never said a word; he flung him out in the direction of the yard like a sack of rubbish and slammed the door.

And there Tailor Molin remained lying. He stayed that way until the Erik Larssons came past—they were Otto Holmberg's nearest neighbors. They had a horse and wagon and they understood immediately what had happened, and they took him home and bandaged him up with compresses and put him to bed and gave him a glass of schnapps. He was there for fourteen days.

And Anton Lundmark told Judith: "Tailor Molin has been having a fight with Otto Holmberg in Finnträsk. They nearly killed each other."

"Is he alive?"

"Which of them?"

"Tailor Molin."

"Yes, he's alive. You need not cry over this, Judith. He's as tough as his dungaree cloth, miserable little creature though he is; they are as hard to kill as an ermine."

And then, after fourteen days, he was so far recovered that he could get up, his legs would bear him, and he began to make his way home.

That day, the same day that Tailor Molin left Erik Larsson's and got as far as Evald Holm's in Avaberg, that was halfway to Inreliden, on that day there was an auction of Elis of Lillåberg's effects. And Anton Lundmark was there, though not Judith, Tailor Molin's Judith: he, Anton Lundmark, didn't want them to appear together among people, and he purchased two wall hangings. "They may come to have some value," he said. "They are, after all, a bit like works of art."

And when he came home he put them on the kitchen table.

It was there Judith found them. She had come from the barn and had warmed the milk for the calves; she was in the habit of stopping with the calves for hours.

She saw immediately what it was that lay on the kitchen table, that it was wall hangings. And she could not control herself. She unrolled them.

LIFE IS PAIN AND PAIN IS ITS OWN FORGIVENESS

and

IT IS GOOD FOR ME TO BE PUNISHED

They were not the best wall hangings he had made, but all the same she remained standing a long time gazing at them as if she had never seen a wall hanging before, he was after all the only person she knew who sewed wall hangings, was Tailor Molin.

When evening came she at last had the courage and strength to refuse Anton Lundmark and say that she did not only need to humble herself, that she had atoned for the destruction she had done and that was why she was seeking to make amends for her transgressions, time after time anew, and that now she intended to seek the true atonement and hold to it forever.

Anton Lundmark believed that she was contrite, so he left her in peace, for contrition—it comes and goes.

The next day, after they had eaten fried porridge and after she had cleared up there in the kitchen, and after she had seen to the calves and washed the separator, she went home to Inreliden. It was a Saturday.

Tailor Molin had just come home, he was sitting inside the door getting back his strength. He appeared to be almost glad when he saw her, he didn't seem taken aback or surprised.

"Is the basket empty now?" he said.

"Yes," she said. "Now the basket is empty."

And she counted out the money he was to have for those wall hangings she had sold, eighteen crowns.

And then she said: "There are hangings that are almost like revelations. There are hangings one can't harden one's heart against."

But she no longer went out selling. Tailor Molin wanted to do that himself, and there were of course those stories of his; people were accustomed to them—in many places they bought his hangings just for the sake of two stories, it didn't matter that they were old stories, that they soon knew them as well as Tailor Molin himself.

One was about Isabella Stenlund and the preacher.

And there were sermons that he said he knew word for word. And people certified that yes, it was word for word.

And about the Nicanors and their horse the north Swedish mare who was called Gloria, not to mention Gabriel Israelsson and his cows, the beautiful Merab in particular.

And the letters he knew by heart; he'd been allowed to read them one single time and he knew them by heart.

One was about Jacob Lundmark and the stump grubber.

And there were stories we have altogether forgotten.

There were many people who went to Judith when they knew that Tailor Molin was away, that he was out with his basket telling stories, and they tried to tempt Judith with schnapps, and they flattered her; people said she was loose-living, and they offered her money, they were bachelors and old men and widowers and married men who, for all that, were alone. But they got nothing for it, they knew nothing about man's soul, they thought it was like a belch.

MAN'S SOUL IS LIKE THE BIRD'S NEST UP IN THE TREE TOP

And when Tailor Molin told his stories that was how they sounded. Just like this.

The Biggest Words

THE preacher lived there at the Stenlunds'. The preacher always lived at the Stenlunds'; they had a special preacher's bed. The Stenlunds had a daughter called Isabella. Isabella Stenlund.

He always began his sermons by saying that he was an ordinary brother, he was in no way remarkable. "I am only here so that together we may talk of what is beyond and what comes from above," he used to say; but that was before he got properly started on his sermon, before the Word got him in its power. He was from Nylund beyond Malå.

The meeting itself used to be held at the Holmgrens; the kitchen there was as large as the portal of a barn, there were plenty of chairs and they had an organ.

He was an unusually handsome preacher, big and tall he was, and people said he had the strength of a giant, one of the sort that the daughters of men bore God's sons at the time before the Flood in the first book of the Bible when men's wickedness flourished; and he had wavy hair, he was brown-eyed, and he made his mustache shiny and black with some sort of cream. Yes, if you have seen Aron Stenlund, the schoolmaster in Risträsk, he who talks so fearfully, the man they are now sending to parliament, then you will know what that preacher looked like, they look like father and son. If only I could remember what he was called, but his name was certainly something beautiful. Preachers usually take new beautiful names.

Isabella Stenlund was no beauty, but she was not particularly ugly either; she had been betrothed to a man from Fårträsk, but it came to nothing, he was drowned timber-floating. She was thin and melancholy. She was thirty-four.

And autumn was far advanced.

When they had been in bed for a long time, there at the Stenlunds', when the old people had already fallen asleep and there was not a light burning in the village; when even Isabella felt that slumber was on the way, she had had to wait for sleep to come, for after all there was a strange man in the house. Then the preacher left the chamber where they had made up a couch for him; he was wearing a long nightshirt of glossy material and he went on tiptoe and walked right through the kitchen to the little chamber where Isabella lay. He shut the door behind him and sat down on the edge of her bed. And she was frightened.

"Don't be frightened," he said.

"I'm not frightened," she said.

"I only need someone to talk to," he said.

"I'm no young girl," said Isabella. "I shall never be frightened again."

"Are you a believer?" he said.

"I believe in God," she said, "but give myself to Him I cannot."

"No?"

"He drowned Hemming, my betrothed, out in the Vorm rapids. And my youth and my happiness He has also taken from me."

"Though His mercy is everlasting," he then said.

But she did not answer.

"I can't sleep," continued the preacher. "It is as if my heavenly father begrudged me sleep."

"If the body is allowed to work itself tired, sleep comes of itself," said Isabella.

"My body wants to sleep sure enough. But the Spirit will not allow it."

"The Spirit," said Isabella.

"The Spirit is like fermenting dough, he presses on me from all sides. He gives me no peace."

"How do you know that it is the Spirit?" she said.

"He talks within me," said the preacher. "I hear him. His voice is tremendous and loud."

He was looking almost miserable, as if he was really being tormented. He screwed up his eyes as if to save her from seeing the suffering in his face. And Isabella laid her hand on his knee; she did not want him to feel quite forsaken.

"It is as if the words were too big," he said. "As if there wasn't really room for them in me."

"What sort of words are they?" she said. And her voice was tender, as if it was a little baby or a decrepit person or a sucking calf she was talking to.

"They are God's words," he said. "Words way beyond the law, the prophets, and the Gospel. And Paul. And the Book of Revelations. And the Catechism."

"Do they really make a noise inside you?" she said.

"Yes," he said. "They thunder and carry on inside me like the gases of digestion. And it's worst at night."

Then she moved an inch nearer to him as if she thought she would be able to hear the words rumbling through his flesh, through the thickness of his flesh.

"Like when one has eaten pea soup," she said.

"Yes," he said.

"Or like an organ," she said.

"Yes, even like an organ."

"Like having an organ inside you!"

"The words carry no fetters," he said. "The words have the force of a gale."

"Yes," she said, "I've sometimes thought about that. That words can be, as it were, wild and ungovernable. So you have to be particular and watchful about them. Those words."

"The biggest words are the worst," he said. "Corruption. And Eternity. And Wild Beast. And Mercy. And Sanctification. And Regeneration. And Beatification. And Redemption. And Original Sin."

"Yes," she said. "Those words are tremendous."

"Not to mention Love," he said.

"Yes," she said. "Love."

And now he crept up into her bed, she let him do it, it was not only the words, he was cold too.

And just as he was creeping up to her, he named two words from the Letter to the Corinthians: Cold and Nakedness.

And he went on counting up words for her, all the big words that were always passing with the thunder of a storm inside his chest, his head, and the whole of his gigantic man's body.

The words lay like a weight upon her. For him they were inside, but she experienced them externally like a burden on her breast; it was as if they wanted to force their way into her, to take possession of her, and she was obliged to get out of bed and stretch and draw a deep breath several times, and shake her arms and hands and shoulders like she did in the mornings to get rid of her sleepiness and dreams. Some nights she dreamed horribly; she did not know whether she was equal to such tremendous words, whether there was room in her for them, but later she crept into bed again.

And he waited for her, he'd seen into her and understood

that she was fighting a battle, and he still had a great many
words left, and a number of those words were only sounds and
not letters and syllables, they were also painful, perhaps they
were the most painful for one never knew for certain what
they meant; and she stroked his wavy hair and said, "Poor
thing, poor thing," as she was in the habit of saying to the
animals to be slaughtered.

"The Spirit and the words and the language won't leave
me in peace until I'm in my grave," he said. "If then."

"The Spirit and the words and the language have no end,
they last forever."

And it even happened that he wept. And she comforted
him right until the morning.

When later on they ate barley porridge before the eleven
o'clock meeting, they sat around the gate-legged table in the
Stenlunds' kitchen, then Isabella told her parents that she had
given herself to God during the night, the words had prevailed
with her. The words that bear fruit.

And the old people seemed pleased.

And then he preached as if inspired and released; he who
has beheld the company of the free he is happy in his work,
this was in the Holmgrens' large kitchen. "In the beginning
was the Word, and the Word was with God. All things were
made by Him and without Him was not anything made that
was made. In Him was life; and the life was the light of men.
And the Word was made flesh."

That is how it was for him: his words were the Word and his
flesh, that was the Flesh.

How things turned out for him afterward I don't know.
Preachers, they come and go, they have no permanence, they
are as fleeting and capricious as the birds of the air and the fish

in the sea, but Isabella got a boy in the spring, she did, and that was the fellow Aron Stenlund, he is a miserable chatterbox, he is, as it were, stuffed full of words, but he is a scholar, and now they are going to send him to Stockholm. And she'll soon be the only one left of the congregation, will Isabella Stenlund; they are dying off little by little.

The Holmgrens who had an organ, they have gone too.

Two Sermons

The Word

THE sower soweth the Word.

"Whoso despiseth the Word shall be destroyed.

"There is that speaketh rashly like the piercings of a sword.

"But the tongue of the wise is healthy."

It is also written: "He sendeth His word and healeth them."

At Storholmträsk there lived a man called Samuel Burvall. He died some years ago at the sanatorium; it was a hemorrhage of the lungs.

It happened like this in his case.

The Burvalls of Storholmträsk had a habit of dying of consumption. Four of his paternal aunts and three of his paternal uncles died when he was a child, also his father's father, and two siblings, the only ones he had, and three cousins.

He worried a lot about this.

People constantly talked about the way consumption traveled across the earth, making its way from person to person. Was it by the fogs of winter, or by cows' milk, or was it in the water, or in the sheepskin coverings that folk lay under, or in their breath, or was it in the knives and forks and spoons that had not been properly washed, and each and every one had their own view. Some were afraid of the fog, others of cows' milk. Some were afraid of the sheepskin rugs, and some of breath, and these bent backward when they talked to anyone, and many people shunned knives and forks and spoons.

But when Samuel Burvall was fourteen he believed he knew the truth of it: that it was the word itself that was the source of the infection, the word *consumption,* and he made up his mind that he would never let that word into his body, he would shut his ears to the sound and letters of it, he would keep his hearing and his senses clean of consumption, just as other people strove for cleanliness in the matter of fleece rugs, and cutlery, and water, and cows' milk, and breath.

Thus when he was with people he sat on tenterhooks, he sat with the palms of his hands against his cheekbones, it looked as if he was in the habit of supporting his head a little, as if it was extremely heavy, and the minute he realized that anyone was about to utter that horrible, contagious word, he quickly stuck his fingers into his ears, so that not a word could get in. That which leaves the mouth comes from the heart, and that is what contaminates people.

It wasn't easy, people were always talking about consumption, there wasn't much else to talk about. Consumption was, as it were, the greatest mystery in the matter of life and death, consumption was like the seven stars in the angel's hand. Therefore watchful and careful and almost unsociable was what Samuel Burvall had to be.

But he was strong and healthy, and when he was nineteen and had to enlist, he had never had the least hint of any trouble. He was felling trees at that time in Vackerliden, and he took his skis and went to Norsjö, and the doctor who examined him said he was like one of David's heroes, he was two ells and an inch around the chest, he was like Elisha, and he weighed ninety-five kilos, all of them only flesh and muscle.

But the thing happened that should never have happened. It was one of the recruiting gentlemen—he had so many shiny buttons and stars you couldn't count them—he looked up from the papers he had before him, and looked at Samuel Burvall, and said: "Well, well, Burvall," to him. And Samuel had no time to defend himself, he was caught quite off his guard, and the recruiting gentleman had a voice he wouldn't anyhow have been able to stop, a voice that would have gone straight through Samuel's hands, and he shouted:

"Have you had consumption, Burvall?"

And he felt that the word had hit him like a bullet, it was as if it had torn a hole in his ear. And he felt the poison from the word spreading through his body and blood. Now it's all over with me, he thought, and he answered the recruiting gentleman thus:

"No, I've not had consumption. Not so far."

And so he was called up; they wanted to make a noncommissioned officer of him. That was in the 20th Infantry in Umeå. But only a few weeks passed after which he fell ill. There was fluid in his pleural cavity and patches on both lungs, and they had to send him back to Storholmträsk.

And the old Burvalls fitted him out for the sanatorium, they weren't badly off. There were suits and nightshirts, and a new Bible, and white shirts and ties and cuff links; they knew what was wanted. And Sofia Lundström from Åmträsk came over to say good-bye. They had been confirmed together, she and Samuel, and there was a sort of understanding between them, so the old Burvalls left them alone, for they also knew from experience what it was like to say good-bye.

He was away for two years.

And when he came home again he was cured. His skin was white and he talked Swedish for the first few days, and a lot of his flesh had fallen away, but he was cured. And the old Burvalls said: "If only he goes back to work."

But he said: "Why should I go back to work? Life is better than work. To work isn't the same thing as to survive."

And the old Burvalls had never heard anything like that before. To live was to get a grip on things, wasn't it, not to spare yourself? But he was the last child they had. Gaffer Burvall himself had had shingles, he had a bad heart and probably hadn't long to live.

Yes, I know that you have all heard much talk about Samuel Burvall, that you already know how things were. But I shall lift him up and bring him forward, and shine a light on him so that the very meaning itself may be revealed. I shall make a sermon out of him.

And Samuel said to the old man:

"This shall never happen again. That word that pushed its way into me and infected me, that shall never henceforth come near my ears, I shall be on my guard so that it may never again take possession of me."

"But how will you do that?" said the old people. "It is one of the commonest words, that word, people say it every day, many can talk of nothing else."

And old Burvall remembered the Epistle to the Romans: "And thinkest thou this, O man . . . that thou shall escape the judgment of God?"

But Samuel Burvall, he did everything in the way he had thought of, everything that he had worked out while he was at the sanatorium. He got timber from Gumboda, and nails and a long iron tube from Norsjö, and a window with two frames joined together from Lycksele; and he did all the building work himself so that it should be as he wanted it. He was very particular and he was not without skill, and what the old man said couldn't be helped.

And Sofia Lundström came. They had exchanged letters while he was at the sanatorium, and she said to him: "You'll soon be a whole man again, Samuel, you'll be like Goliath, you'll soon take over the farm and be your own master."

And he understood immediately what she meant.

"Why are you setting a trap for my life?" he said. "Strength, and the farm, and being one's own master are trifles, a puff of wind compared with having life itself."

"We must weave life to the end," she said. "We must not let the loom stand idle. It has been said: 'We must both die and live with each other.' "

"But one must never die unnecessarily," he said. "I was near to death, Sofia. To die is to be like water."

"But you're well now," she said. "You no longer have that illness, that suffering, that weakness."

She saw how terrified he became when she said this, and how he screwed up his eyes, and how his lips began to tremble. He was afraid that she might thoughtlessly and, as it were, in haste, speak that word, and when she observed this she felt that she could almost have burst into tears.

"I shall never say anything you can't endure to hear," she said, "Not a single word."

"It isn't that I'm fragile or oversensitive," he said. "But I can't resist infection."

"No," she said. "If only you could resist infection."

"That's right," he said. "Then I should have taken over the farm. Then I should have wanted to have you, Sofia." And then he continued: "Though we can always talk to each other. I should like us always to be able to talk to each other."

And he moved into the little room he had built, and he had insulated the walls and put in a double window, and he had a hatch in the wall over the top of the ladder where he received the food they prepared for him, and which the maid carried up to him. She was called Eline and came from Kvavisträsk. And there through that same hatch he put out the slop pail that had to be emptied evening and morning. He was particular about the time, he lived like a clock.

And he had pushed the iron tube, a one-inch tube it was, he had pushed it with its head by his bed down into the kitchen so that the orifice was by the cowl over the hearth, and if you sat on the woodbox you could talk right into the tube. I myself was allowed to try to talk to him once, I was preaching in Lillholmträsk, and it wasn't far away. And I said to him: "Samuel, Samuel. 'Mercy unto you and grace and peace and love be multiplied,' " it was the Epistle of Jude, but he didn't hear me, he never answered, perhaps he had a cork in the upper end. Through that tube he talked to Hanna, his mother, Hanna Burvall, and to Sofia, but never to a stranger.

People have often asked what in fact he did there, what he got up to in that little room in the attic, how things were for him. And I answer:

"He lived.

"He lived in safety.

"He was preserved."

After two years had passed old Burvall died, and Hanna told Samuel through that iron tube: "Papa died last night."

"Yes," he said, "I saw it by his looks—that he wouldn't last long."

"It's more than two years since you saw him," Hanna told him.

"What are two years?" he said. "Two years are like a breath of wind."

"He rebuilt the wall of the stove in the cowshed," said Hanna.

"He got ready the wood for winter.

"He marked out the new pasture by Elof's field.

"He delivered Pärla when she was about to die giving birth to a calf.

"He built new steps down to the cellar.

"And he went to Lycksele to exchange the horse.

"And he made a new beam for the loom.

"And he kept the ice from the cellar.

"That's what he did these last two years," said Hanna.

"Well," said Samuel, "what ought he to have done? And after all he had a weak heart."

"We are going to bury him on Sunday."

"It's all the same to me," said Samuel. "People talk so unluckily at funerals."

And so.

After that life was pretty hard for Hanna Burvall on her own with only the maid to help her and Samuel up in the attic. But he comforted her: "I'm here up in my room. If you can't sleep at night, or if you have a pain anywhere, or if you want someone to talk to, you'll know that I'm here."

"Yes," she said. "I'll always know where to find you."

People asked Eline, the maid: "What does he look like, does he cut his hair and his beard?" And she told them the truth of it. "I don't know. I empty his slop pail, and I give him his food. He eats well, and his stomach works as it should, but I never see him, no one has seen him since he locked the door. It's a lock with two keyholes."

That's how things really were. For all those years there was no one who saw Samuel Burvall.

And on Sundays Sofia Lundström sat on the woodbox by the cowl over the hearth in the Burvalls' kitchen and talked to him between twelve o'clock coffee and dinnertime. And she told him about all that she had been doing and everything she had heard people talking about, but the name of that illness she never uttered. It was as if consumption did not exist, as if that suffering was at an end forever, though during those years three of the Lundgrens of Avabäck died of it, and one Stenlund of Lakaträsk, and three of Samuel's own cousins, and they could sit in silence for long periods. All the same they seemed to belong to each other. That iron tube was like a link or a bond between them, and she never had another man. People knew that she was Samuel Burvall's Sofia. They were almost like man and wife.

And that was probably the cause of his misfortune.

As it says in Ecclesiastes: "Two are better than one; because they have a good reward for their labors."

And as the prophet Amos says: "Can two walk together except they be agreed?"

He asked her about many things and of course she sometimes thought he asked peculiar questions. But she was patient, and she never said to him: "You could very well come out and see for yourself." She answered as if he was really blind, or lay paralyzed in his bed.

"If you stand on the bridge can you see Ormberg?

"How many panes of glass are there in the gable of the cowshed?

"Are there two or are there three chimneys on Elof Lindström's house?

"If it blows from the east does the weather vane on the bakehouse roof move?

"Is the tree that stands this side of the forest a birch, or is it a big sallow?

"When the aspens shed their leaves as now, are they yellow, or are they red?"

"They are red."

And when they killed an animal at the Lundströms' in Amträsk she usually took with her a piece of roast meat; he was very fond of roast meat.

And she read sermons for him, and sometimes, if he felt he had time, also from the Book of Homilies, that is to say from Luther's homilies.

And he told her whether he had slept well or badly, what he'd been thinking about during the last few days, the birds he'd seen through the window, also the weather he'd noticed, indeed everything that had happened since they last talked to each other, yes everything.

"What an awful lot the swallows are flying."

But there was something wrong with Sofia.

After five years had passed it happened that on one Sunday she did not come.

"Man that is born of woman is of few days and is full of trouble." He does not know what will come to pass, and who can tell him what will come to pass? No man has mastery over the wind to check it.

"I wonder whether Sofia won't make her way here today?" Samuel said to Hanna through the tube. "It's Sunday, isn't it?"

"She's probably sitting at her loom," said Hanna. "Or she may be at the slaughtering at Lakaberg. And she always knows where she can find you."

"But she said nothing about anything special last Sunday," he said.

"Or perhaps she has moved," said Hanna. "She is quite free. To Lycksele or Umeå."

"She would never leave me. Not Sofia."

"You're silly," she told him. "You're silly in the way small children are."

"It's true, there's much I don't know. But that I do know. I know it for certain."

And Sofia had a sort of feeling of unease inside her. On some Sundays she only wanted to laugh and make fun of him. She was the way she had been at the time they went to confirmation classes with the parson. On other Sundays she was mostly silent, said nothing about the towels she was weaving, or about a cow that had calved, or about betrothals or marriages that she'd seen about in the papers, or of the children who were always being born both here and there. And her voice was so weak that he had to shout, "Sofia, Sofia," time after time.

And he never dared to ask: "Why do you sound so gloomy, Sofia?"

And she had developed that cough.

It was that dry, hacking cough, and you could hear that she was holding her hand in front of her mouth, and that she was breathing short, careful breaths, so that the cough shouldn't get the better of her completely, and that she was sucking peppermint sweets so that he should smell the odor through the tube, but he never dared to ask: "Have you got a cough, Sofia?"

And Hanna warned him. "I believe that Sofia isn't very strong, Samuel."

But Samuel said: "If she will only eat properly. Barley meal porridge. And meat."

And people told her: "You should try to do something about your cough, Sofia. You should go to the doctor."

But she wouldn't hear of it.

"When I'm alone I never cough," she said. "But when I'm with people I cough."

Thus said the Moabitess Ruth: "Entreat me not to leave thee, or to return from following thee: for whither thou goest I will go; and where thou lodgest I will lodge: thy people shall be my people, and thy God my God.

"Where thou diest I will die, and there will I be buried: The Lord do so unto me, and more so if aught but death do part thee and me."

* * *

And at last the Lundströms of Åmträsk had to get themselves a maid, though they couldn't really afford one, they had so little forest, and only four cows, but all the same Sofia had grown too weak. She had to rest in the middle of the day. "I'll just get up my strength for a bit," she said; and she had red patches on her cheeks, and her handkerchief had what looked like spots of rust on it, and she never went to the sewing bees anymore.

And the sort of weakness she had was perfectly clear, the affliction that had befallen her, what she was suffering from.

Though on most Sundays she got herself to Storholm-träsk. Old Lundström used to drive her there, he said: "I'm sure I'll get a cup of coffee from Hanna Burvall. She may be glad to spend some time chatting. She is, as it were, alone.

"So we've both got an errand there you and I, Sofia."

The last time, in May that was, and there was hardly any snow left, and old Lundström had wrapped her up in sheepskin rugs, and he had to carry her, she had no strength left in her legs. That was the spring she turned thirty-two. Samuel had then been living up in his room for seven years. And old Lundström carried her in and sat her on the woodbox, and drew aside the sheepskin rugs.

And Samuel was so uneasy and fearful that he could hardly manage to sit still beside the iron tube. His teeth were chattering and his whole body was shaking. He could hear by her voice that she was quite done in, and he realized that she had to summon up all the strength she had left in order to sit there and talk to him. She hadn't breath for the words she wanted to utter. She's near death, he thought. She's going to give me up.

And he said: "Have you sheared the sheep yet, Sofia?"

"Yes, of course we've sheared the sheep."

"And you've baked the flat loaves?"

"Yes, both the flat loaves and the thin bread."

"And the scrubbing? The big house?"

"Yes, we're doing it. We'll soon be scrubbed up ready for the summer."

"And the slaughtering? The spring slaughtering?"

"Yes, we've killed the pig, and two yearling lambs."

"You mustn't overwork, Sofia."

"Don't fret, Samuel. We have a maid now. Fretting isn't good for you, it can become a sort of illness."

"And the old people?"

"They sent you a bit of meat. Dried lamb's meat."

After that she was two weeks in bed at Åmträsk, and finally the old Lundströms sent for the doctor. He gave her opium tablets and said she was going through a crisis, but that it was too late, and that it was a disgrace that they hadn't sent for help earlier.

"What is the good of science if people continue to rely on their own doubtful abilities?"

But the truth was that it had been too late for two years, yes for the whole time. And who can know for certain that she wanted to live?

When Hanna, Hanna Burvall, heard that she was dead— it was old Lundström who came there to tell her—then she thought, Anyway it's unavoidable, someone must tell him, and now I'm the only person left in the world who can talk to him. And she went to the woodbox and sat on it, and she sat there for a good long time holding on to the mantelpiece of the stove, and she said to the maid Eline: "You can go out and see if the calves are in the enclosure." And she was so full of dread that her face seemed paralyzed, and what her lips desired gave her no relief. And she bent forward and put her mouth to the tube and called: "Samuel, Samuel."

And he answered: "Yes, here I am."

And then she told him. "Sofia has died. She died last night."

He said nothing. There was complete silence in the tube, you couldn't even hear him breathing. And so she said again: "Sofia died last night."

Of course he heard what she said, but to hear is not to understand, it took time for the words to eat their way into him, it was as it is when a fever pierces through a human being. He thought, I'm losing my reason. And inside him it was as black as night, and he took hold of the iron tube to save himself from collapsing, and he thought, I've talked to her, haven't I? I've talked to her every Sunday. I talked to her only a few weeks ago. Death can't come suddenly like that. She was scrubbing up for the summer, wasn't she?

Though after a time he saw that it was true all the same. Why should Hanna think up a thing like that? And Sofia had been ill for a long time, there was that hacking cough and her breathlessness, and he remembered that he had thought that she was going to abandon him, he'd half thought so, but had not dared to ask her, hadn't wanted to risk his life by asking her, if only he'd at least asked her, and then he thought, It doesn't matter anymore. Now everything is over. Why should I be bound to life like a fetus in the womb? Now there is no longer a word that I fear.

And he put his mouth to the iron tube and shouted in despair, shouted so that it thundered through Hanna's kitchen: "Was it consumption? Was it consumption that took Sofia?"

And Hanna said: "Yes, it was consumption."

Eline had now come back, and after a while they heard that he was unlocking the door, using both the keys, and they heard him come down the stairs. He moved like one who is slow and stiff, it sounded like old Burvall in his last years, and then he came down to them. He had stuffed his long beard into his trouser waistband, and his hair hung down over his shoulders. He stepped into the kitchen, and Hanna scanned his face, saw how he had aged, how he was suffering. And she thought, He won't fight against it anymore, his eyes are quite blank, he's in despair; he's at once doomed and set free.

And she said to him: "Consumption is only an illness, Samuel. Some die of it, others don't. But all the same it's only an illness."

It's true.

And thus saith King Solomon:

"A man's belly shall be satisfied with the fruit of his mouth, and with the increase of his lips shall he be filled.

"Death and life are in the power of the tongue . . ."

Mercy

I remember a soul that I saved.

He was called Lundgren and was a native of Granträskliden.

Through the word cometh mercy unto us.

It was after a meeting in Lakaberg, there in the Holmgrens' kitchen. He had come there as a farmhand, he was a stranger. In the winter he chopped wood for charcoal. Getting on for forty he was, and unmarried; he seemed rather meditative and had coal-black hair and brown eyes like those the Lundgrens of Granträskliden always have. In the summer he had dug a well for the Holmgrens. It was twenty-five feet deep and he dug it without help and it has never run dry. That's what he was like. And I remember that we sang: "Oh, thou bitter well of sorrow, oh thou wretched sinful body, how shall our hearts thee satisfy."

He sat over by the pantry door, behind all the others, he sat looking down at the floor. And I looked at him and thought, He only wants company for a while, he does not look like a man who wants salvation.

But when all the others had gone—they went quietly and carefully, their souls were bowls of the waters of life—he sat where he was by the pantry door. And I went up to him.

And I remember that I said: "Are you longing to clothe yourself in the garment of salvation?"

Then he looked up and looking up at me, said: "If only it was enough to long."

"But it is still a beginning," I said.

"I can see redemption before me," he said. "But I shall not be able to enter therein."

He sat holding out the palms of his hands and looked at them; they were large and sort of rough.

"Our Lord has you in mind," I said. "He has everyone in mind."

And I drew up a chair and sat down beside him. This will take time, I thought.

"I'm stuck fast in the devil's snare," he said. "The devil has his dwelling in my heart."

"Yes," I said. "It may seem like that. But it is only contrition."

"Contrition?" he said.

"Our heart is contrite," I said. "And then it feels just like the devil."

But then he said: "I am not contrite. I am calm and in full control. And I am at the height of my powers."

He is obdurate, I thought. The sword has not gone through his soul, he lacks the right understanding, his heart is hardened, he only knows about wood for charcoal and digging wells.

"You can't win salvation without a struggle," I said.

"If it was only that," he said and looked at his great hands. "If it was only a struggle."

"Yes," I said. "It's a matter of fighting the good fight of faith." Then I described the laws of mercy to him, the laws of mercy that men must know by heart, though in these parts it isn't common. One must never leave anything to chance.

"The call, when the Word seizes hold of you and shakes you.

"Enlightenment, when the Spirit holds out its light toward your sin.

"Regeneration, when Our Lord opens your eyes and bestows life on you once more.

"Conversion, when he fills you with his will, and helps you to forget what you yourself want.

"Righteousness, when Our Lord endows you with belief so that you become righteous.

"Sanctification, when he obliterates the sin in your heart.

"Steadfastness, when the Spirit holds you fast so that you don't run off in all directions.

"Blessedness, when the Spirit tells you: 'Now the struggle is over, now everything will be made clear to you.' "

"Yes," he said. "For some people it is as simple and painless as that."

"But for you the laws of mercy are impossible?" I said.

"Yes," he said. "Even if I use force I can't penetrate the laws of mercy."

"But what if you have help?" I said.

"And if you also used force?" he said.

"Where the laws of mercy are concerned one must not be considerate," I said. "It is a struggle for life or death."

"You must not be too sure," he said, and looked hard at me. "Sometimes even a preacher may be at a loss."

"Where the laws of mercy are concerned, there is no pardon," I said.

"And the meeting is over," he said. "Both the meeting and what comes after. You may need to rest. Your sermon was like a good day's work for a man."

"Nothing," I said. "Nothing I need to rest from if I can save a soul."

"And you've had no food," he said. "No evening meal."

"I can eat cold porridge," I said. "If I can save a soul I shall eat cold porridge with joy in my heart."

And then at last he told me how things were.

"I went to sea," he said. "I went to sea for four years. We plied between Holmsund and Stockholm with timber, and between Stockholm and Holmsund with earth and stones, it was called ballast. The last trip we did we had to take on board some barrels of tar in Örnskjöldsvik. We stayed there for the night and I went ashore; it wasn't particularly amusing on the boat, and I was like a tall-growing sapling. I could not just lie on my back in my bunk.

"And I met a man who sold clocks and razors and silver rings. He had schnapps and I bought a knife from him, a knife to clean my nails with. And we chatted together; he was born in Glommerträsk, so it was almost as if he came from home, and we sat ourselves down on a bench down below Strandgatan, opposite the town park; I remember it as if it was yesterday; and he said:

" 'I can make clocks go backward.'

" 'Indeed,' I said.

" 'You don't believe me,' he said.

" 'No,' I said. 'If clocks are sound, they go in the same direction as time.'

"He had a little gold ring in his right ear and a parti-colored neckerchief under his shirt, and his hair was black and curly; he was a bit like a gypsy, and it seemed as if he was offended that I didn't believe him.

" 'The world is not as simple as North-Sea dwellers believe,' he said. 'There is more between heaven and earth than North-Sea dwellers have dreamt of.'

" 'Time goes forward,' I said. 'Therefore clocks go forward too.'

" 'For the most part that is so,' he said. 'But not always.'

" 'Though if you turn the cogwheel around,' I said, 'then it will go backward.'

" 'You think that I am a braggart,' he said. 'Some sort of cheat.'

" 'I believe that God watches over the ordering of his creation,' I said."

And I said this to him as we sat down there by the pantry door: "You were right. The ear shall test the words and the mouth the taste of what you want to eat. And if one has doubts about God's laws, then one has doubts about God too."

We were quite alone in the big kitchen, it was the middle of summer so the Holmgrens were living in the bakehouse; the people who had been at the meeting were down by the bridge, chatting.

And Lundgren, the man who was born in Granträskliden and who had been at sea and whom I was fighting to save, he continued:

"Then that clock trickster in Örnskjöldsvik took out a watch from his inside pocket. And he held it out to me and said: 'Take this.'

"And I took the watch, and he told me to examine it, that it was going as it should and that he had not turned the cogwheel around and that the watchcase was sound and that it was wound up properly.

"It was a pocket watch and it was called Norma, and it was saying a quarter to eleven in the evening and I held it against my ear and it ticked and went so that the case tinkled good and proper.

"And he said: 'Hold it out on the palm of your hand.'

"And I did.

"And he held out his right hand and ran his finger backward and forward a couple of times over the watch without touching it, and he shut his eyes and his face twitched as if he had a cramp, and he pursed his mouth and seemed to chew. It was as if he was saying something that wasn't to be heard.

"And after a bit he said: 'Look now and see what time it is.'

"And now it was twenty to eleven.

"And I said this to him: 'It has gone five minutes backward. You've taken it to pieces.'

" 'I can make it turn back when I like,' he said.

" 'What did you do to the watch?' I said.

" 'I adjusted it. My hands are magnetic.'

" 'Magnetic!' I said.

" 'Yes,' he said. 'Magnetic.' "

Now the people who had been at the meeting had gone home; they were not standing by the bridge anymore; many of them had small children of course, and could not be away too long. And I thought, It's hard for him to believe, something has happened to him that makes him unable really to believe, this fellow Lundgren. But it can't be just this business with the watch.

"No one can have magnetic hands," I said. "That would be supernatural. And the supernatural doesn't exist. Except, of course, where religion is concerned," I added.

"That's what I told him," Lundgren now said. "That's what I told that clock trickster in Örnskjöldsvik. 'No one can have magnetic hands.'

" 'I can't help that,' he said. 'I say the same as you: no one should need to have magnetic hands.'

"It sounded as if he had mixed feelings about it. He took out the schnapps and we drank a drop, and the watch went on going backward, very soon it was only ten-thirty.

" 'Do you believe me now?' he said.

" 'Yes,' I said. 'I believe.'

"For I had seen it with my own eyes.

" 'But I can't understand what you do,' I said. 'What the trick is.'

" 'It's no trick,' he said. 'It's only some sort of miracle.'

" 'Miracle?' I said. 'Only Our Lord can work those. And I can't see why He should bother Himself to do one of those with a pocket watch, they are such ordinary things. They are only springs and cogwheels and balance wheels.'

"And then he said: 'It's not only pocket watches. If it was only pocket watches, that would be simple.'

" 'Is it pendulum clocks too?' I said. 'Wall clocks?'

"But he didn't like me teasing him. He raised his head and looked at me, and his eyes were black and his mouth sort of twisted. And then he said: 'It's time itself. Time that watches must keep track of.'

"But then I said: 'No. Not time.'

" 'Yes,' he said. 'Time.'

" 'You blaspheme,' I said. 'Time is God's tool. Time is God's passage through the world when he creates.'

" 'If you will lend me your watch,' he said, 'then I will turn back your time for you.'

" 'Never,' I said.

" 'You will go backward down to your boat,' he said, 'and the boat will go back to Holmsund stern first, and when morning comes you will go to bed and you will again unload the boat of timber in Holmsund.'

" 'And Grandfather who died a month ago?' I asked.

" 'They will dig him up and he will rise up from his coffin again.'

" 'If you tamper with time then you are a dead man,' I said. 'He who turns back time, he has not the right to live.' "

I saw that the Holmgrens came out and stood on the bakehouse steps; they looked toward the windows of the big kitchen; they were asking themselves how long it was going to take to save that man Lundgren. After all he was their farmhand.

"Yes," I said to him. "That was only right. He who believes he can change the course of time, he is not fit to live. He who abuses and reviles time, he is a blasphemer."

But that man Lundgren, he had not finished yet.

" 'I know so little about God,' said that clock trickster. 'But if He is like time, then He is pretty unpredictable.'

" 'God,' I said, 'He is like the almanac and the heavenly bodies, without Him there is no stability or certainty.'

" 'How can you know that?' said the clock trickster.

" 'That's what I've learned,' I said. 'And that's how it's always been. That God has seen to it that there should be law and order.'

" 'Give me your watch,' he said.

" 'Never,' I said. 'You shall never have my watch.'

" 'You don't dare,' he said.

" 'Ought I to be afraid of you?' I said.

" 'There is something you're afriad of,' he said. And it was not without a trace of a sneer.

" 'It is called Omega,' I said. 'And I got it from Grandfather when I was fifteen.'

" 'Yes,' he said. 'They are good watches. They are called branded watches.'

" 'So they never . . .' I said.

"And I looked to see what the watch was saying, the watch he had bewitched; it was nearly ten but from the wrong direction. And he sat holding out his hand waiting for me to give him my watch. The Omega.

" 'I just want to look at it,' he said. 'I won't do anything to it. You need not be uneasy.'

" 'You're not going to touch it,' I said.

"He took out the schnapps again, he had it inside his coat, and he held out the bottle to me.

" 'No,' I said. 'I won't have any more schnapps.'

" 'Just a little drop,' he said.

" 'No,' I said, 'it's night already. And my boat goes before seven.'

" 'Only to let me see that you are not easily scared and cowardly,' he said. 'To let me see that you trust me. So you can let me have the Omega. It really is an Omega?'

" 'I don't trust you,' I said.

" 'No,' he said, 'you don't trust anything. And you're right not to. There is nothing that is worthwhile trusting. Not a single living person. And no forces or powers.' And there was mockery in his voice.

" 'You are a blasphemer,' I said. 'You refresh yourself with derision. And Grandfather would not have liked me to lend you my watch,' I added. 'If he had been alive.'

"But then he said: 'If you really believed in your Creator then you would give me your watch.'

" 'I fear my Creator,' I said.

" 'Yes,' he said. 'That may well be so. But you have understood what creation is really like, and that's why you are afraid: that creation is like the works of a watch, and can run in whichever direction it pleases. It only needs someone to have magnetic hands, or for there to be something wrong with a cogwheel or a spring or the balance wheel. There is no thought, no intention, no meaning in existence.'

"And while the clock trickster said this he held out his hand and tried to get at my Omega which I kept in an inside pocket; it was as if he believed that I should give way when I saw that creation was as treacherous and unpredictable as the works of a watch; and I grew, as it were, blinded, I grew so furious that everything went black, and my head shook and I couldn't say a word, and my hands clenched so that I could hardly open them, it was like a cramp. It was rage. I was blind, deaf, and dumb with rage."

I saw that the Holmgrens had gone in and shut the door of the bakehouse; they no doubt saw that it was impossible to save this fellow Lundgren and that it would soon be night.

"Dearly beloved brother," I said, and I felt a pang in my heart, for nothing comes without love and pain, love and pain are like firewood and oil for salvation. "Beloved brother," I said, "the godless man's mouth is greedy for wrong. Punishments are prepared for those who mock and blows for the backs of madmen.

"Your rage, that was holy indignation."

But Lundgren did not hear me, he only looked at his hands, his big hands, and he said:

"And I stretched out my arms and took hold of him and lifted him up and he was as light as a puppy that you are beating; and I held him up before me with outstretched arms, and said, 'There's a devil inside you,' and I shook him so that the watches in his pockets rattled, and I saw by his mouth that there was something he was trying to say, but I heard nothing. I was just so filled up by that rage and I had no idea even of how it had sprung up in me; 'an Omega that I got from Grandfather,' I said, and that rage gave me a cramp, something cut into my shoulders and at my back like a jackknife, and I squeezed him together between my hands so that he grew blue in the face, and his head swung backward and forward like a rag doll's.

"Though at last I was forced to put him down. And then he began to defend himself. He lowered his head and drove it into my stomach so that I felt blood in my mouth, and he scratched my face and put his knee into my belly so that it felt as if something broke in pieces, and I had to throw up. I heard

him say: 'It's you who have the devil inside you,' and he kicked
my legs and beat my chest with the small of his hands.

"So then I said: 'Either you or I. Either you or I.'

"And I lifted him up and carried him to one of the
warehouses, it was a harbor warehouse; and I carried him
before me with outstretched arms, and it was no good his
screaming or kicking. 'God watches over the ordering of His
work,' I said, and I sat him down by the warehouse wall, it
was red brick, and I hit him with my fists so that the skin of
my knuckles split.

"You've got to learn that violation of eternal and everlasting right does not go unpunished, I thought. And while I
banged and hit him I heard the watches scrunch into pieces in
his pockets."

"You were possessed by zeal," I said to Lundgren. "Sometimes
we can be consumed by zeal. And one day the whole earth will
be consumed by the zeal of the Lord."

"And toward the end I had to hold him up with my right hand
and only hit him with my left," said Lundgren. "His legs gave
way under him, and his head banged against the brick wall so
that it sounded the way it does when one is chopping wood.
'God's law will last forever and ever,' I said, and the last blow
I gave was such as to tear him loose from my right hand and
he collapsed like an empty sack and there was a jangling of
broken watches as he tumbled down the hill. And he just lay
there.

"After a time I realized that he was dead. That I had
beaten the life out of him. Then I went to the police station,
I think it was just behind the church, and I told the police
about it. 'I've killed a man, he's lying there by the harbor
warehouse. He declared that he could make time go backward,
he said there was no law and order in God's creation, I killed

him with my fists only, now he won't be able to do anything more.' "

"Yes," I said to Lundgren who was seeking salvation, "you couldn't have done anything else. No one should try to wriggle out of justice. We must wear justice like a mantle.

"But the clock trickster was by no means entirely guilt-less. He should never have said that about God and time that He has created. If he had not made fun of the order of things in the world, you would not have needed to kill him. So quite free of guilt he certainly was not.

"And you mustn't believe that you are beyond mercy just because you have killed a fellow human being.

"God's mercy has been made manifest in the salvation of all men. All flesh shall see God's salvation.

"Our Lord makes no exceptions, not even for a man killer."

"And there was a court case," said Lundgren, and now he spoke so softly that it was almost difficult to hear him.

"They said it was murder. And I didn't contradict them. 'Unpremeditated,' they said, and that was certainly true too. And one of the jurors, he was called Lindström and came from Sidensjö, he asked if I regretted it, and then I said:

" 'No.'

"And then they fell sort of silent, but they did not ask anything else.

"And I got prison.

"But when everything was over, when I had got my sentence and they were taking me out of the room, then the judge came up to me, his name was Vigren and he was called the district judge; and he looked at me intently and then he said:

" 'The devil that you have inside you, Lundberg, is one that you will never get rid of. The devil of arrogance and rage.'

"And I knew right away that he was speaking the truth.
"It was as if this was the final verdict. The verdict that
will last forever. That devil I have inside me, inside my breast,
I shall come to have it there as long as I live. That was the real
verdict. And that verdict, it is for life. So that mercy is something I can never reach. There is a verdict between me and
mercy."

So that was the way things stood for this man, Lundgren. Now
I knew how it was. Now was the time for the true struggle
for salvation.

"That's not the way it is with devils," I said. "No human
being can have the same devil in his breast for his whole life.
Devils are like the birds of the air and the fish of the sea, they
come and go, and go and come, they have no permanent
resting place. And the human breast is like a shred of timber;
it is full of cracks and holes, nothing is put there forever. The
human breast is not airtight, the wind blows right through it."

"But I know him," said Lundgren now. "I feel that the
devil of rage is within me still."

And he looked intently at me, his eyes were coal-black,
it was as if he wanted to let me see that that devil was to be
found in his gaze too.

I did not drop my eyes but said: "Those devils we have
within us, they change from day to day, from moment to
moment. It's just a matter of not becoming their slaves, but of
driving them out bit by bit. The devil of envy, and the devils
of adultery and rage, and the devil of cunning. And the backward-looking devil and the devil of self-pity."

"The backward-looking devil?" said Lundgren.

"Yes," I said. "Backward, that's a point of the compass
at which one should not look unless one is obliged to. Except
in the matter of sin, of course."

"If it were just sin," he said.

"The thing that you believe is the devil, that is only enlightenment," I said. "It is that you see your sin."

Now he said nothing for quite a long time.

"Are you sure of that?" he said at last.

"Yes," I said. "I am quite sure. It is like amen in church."

He looked up at me and I saw in his eyes that a light was beginning to dawn on him. And I thought, The time is come for him to have a tiny presentiment about mercy itself. "Regeneration," I said. "And that judge, that district judge, Vigren, he was known far and wide to talk nonsense. He was a braggart."

Actually, I have never heard that Vigren mentioned, I had never heard his name before, but I wanted Lundgren to know how mercy might taste. It is the Word that will save us. Or the words. It is the words that will save us.

"Everyone knew that," I said. "What he said was nothing to go by."

"Is that true?" said Lundgren, and he almost had tears in his eyes.

"Yes," I said. "It is the absolute truth. He was a drivel-monger. A leaky sieve. And a chatterbox."

"And you are certain that it was Vigren?" said Lundgren. "The district judge?"

"Yes," I said. "And that stuff about the devil, he said that to everyone he sentenced."

"Every single one?" said Lundgren.

"Yes," I said. "Without exception. Pickpockets and illicit distillers, and poachers, and adulterers. The lot."

"Did he really say they had the devil inside them?"

"Yes," I said. "It was quite simply a bad habit he had."

And now you could see how regeneration and conversion were beginning to come to him; his hands relaxed and hung down without his bothering about them, and the skin of his face was smooth, and his shoulders sank down a trifle, almost as if he was about to experience some sort of peace; and he shut his eyes so that I should not see his tears.

But just then, just as the wind of conversion was blowing through his breast, just as the spirit of belief was touching his senses, just then I made a mistake. I said: "And that clock trickster in Örnskjöldsvik. He couldn't turn back time. Time is irreversible."

It was a mistake to say this, it was like pouring water on the fire of salvation.

Lundgren's face suddenly darkened again, and he lifted up his hands and I saw that they were shaking. And he said: "You don't believe me."

And then I made another mistake. I said: "He was only pulling your leg. He had been out in the world and learned a thing or two. It was foolish of you to take him seriously."

"Foolish?" said that fellow Lundgren.

"Yes," I said. "Foolish."

And then he said: "It is written: 'Whosoever shall say thou fool, shall be in danger of hellfire.' "

"Yes," I said. "But it is also written: 'The truth shall make you free.' That's why I am telling you the truth. Time, that God has created, always goes in the same direction and flows into eternity."

"That may be," he said, and now he was talking pretty loudly, "but that clock trickster in Örnskjöldsvik, he would have managed to turn time back if I had not done him to death."

"Never," I said. "Never time."

And I saw by the looks of him that now it was really a question of conversion; he clenched his hands so that his knuckles were white, red streaks appeared in his eyes, he straightened his back and stuck out his chest, so that the material around the buttons of his shirt crackled.

"We shall have to settle this," he said. "We must go outside and decide it all."

"Yes," I said. "We haven't any choice."

And we got up and stood for a bit facing each other; and he looked at me fixedly and said: "That is if preachers have any strength except in their tongues."

But then I said: "You don't know what strength is."

There were once some people in Lillholmträsk who believed that preachers couldn't be other than weaklings. But then I took the New Testament which was bound with leather, and I tore it into two bits as if it had been a daily paper.

And when we got outside there was dew on the grass and complete quiet except for a screech owl. Then Lundgren said: "You mustn't think I'm as easily saved as those who are just about worn out."

We went behind the house. We did not want the Holmgrens to hear us; we both knew that this would be long and hard, and the Holmgrens were no longer young and needed their sleep.

First he tried to kick me in my tender parts, he jumped up and stuck out his leg when he was in the air, it was something he had learned to do when he was at sea; but I too had learned a thing or two, so I dodged and got hold of his foot and pulled it so that he fell backward. But he was soon up again and now he took to his fists; he aimed at my eyes and my throat, he knew how much I depended on my throat, but I defended myself with the palms of my hands and my elbows, and now and then I gave him a kick on the shin, just to calm him down, but he hit heavily and hard so that it hurt, and he kept his head down, so that it was impossible to get at him, and he groaned and wailed with rage, the rage of the devil. And no doubt that was why he did not kill me, he was, as it were, wild and mad with rage, but I was calm and calculating, I knew his intentions and plans, it was all part of the rules, and

I told him so as I took a couple of steps backward, and held up my arms in front of me. I told him: "No man can remove or escape God's law," and I heard him reply with Paul, he groaned out the words between his blows: " 'Thou art a whited wall and I shall smite thee.' "

And I said: "Purification from sin is a fearful struggle."

Then he replied, and he hit at me without pause, and now it was the first letter to the Corinthians: " 'Them that are without God judgeth' " and his fists were like ax hammers and his arms like the branches of a great fir tree when there is a storm.

But finally I could feel his blows getting weaker and I stopped backing away from him and tried myself to strike a few blows and he was, as it were, taken off his guard, and I said: " 'Thou shalt not know what hour shall come upon thee.' " And he knew the Book of Revelations too, for he said: " 'I am no angel of Sardis's Church.' "

And I got in a tremendous blow in the middle of his nose so that he stopped dead and stood still, and then I quickly got hold of his arms and twisted him around so that I got behind his back, and when I had him in reverse, as it were, I flung my arms around him and clasped my hands in front of his chest so that he was locked in and captured, but then he bent forward and tossed me with his back so that we both fell facedown, though I did not loose my grip—one must never loose one's grip. And he kicked my shins with his heels, so that I was obliged to draw back my feet and knees, and I squeezed his chest so that I could hear he could hardly breathe; I couldn't bear the thought that he might be lost, a man like that, and we rolled about like small boys do when they fight, and as we spun around like that in the wet grass I saw that Holmgren, old Holmgren, had come out and stood there watching us, he'd come out so that there should be a witness there when Lundgren was saved; and now I summoned up my last strength, I hurled myself with my whole weight against him, and twisted him around and got him under me, and I pressed my forehead against the nape of his neck and pushed his head down onto the ground so that he could not move, and I said:

"Will you give up now, will you hand yourself over?"

But he said nothing, he didn't try to speak; and I let go with my right hand and seized hold of his wrist and pulled his arm onto his back and twisted it around half a turn and then I said:

"Are you prepared to accept mercy?"

But he remained silent; he was breathing quite horribly, so that I was obliged to twist his arm another half turn, and I waited a bit, then I said: "Now you have justification within your reach, Lundgren. And sanctification. Will you give up your resistance and submit?"

Then he lay silent for quite a long time and just struggled. It was a fight for eternal life.

But later, at the end, I could feel him relaxing within my arms and giving up. "Yes," he said with his face down in the earth. "I give up, I want mercy." It was justification, he accepted the word, and I heard old Holmgren shouting, "Alleluia." Lundgren grew suddenly limp and lifeless, like a sleeper. It was reconciliation that was filling him, the peace that suffuses a human being when the Spirit of salvation is blown into his soul and the law of mercy begins its work.

Gloria

THE Nicanors had lived in the same way through all the years. There were eight of them. Nicanor and Althea and their children. The eldest boy, Einar, was twenty-two, the smallest girl, Agnes, was seven. After Agnes it was the end.

And people said to Nicanor: "Have you lost your strength? Only six children and you've given up already?"

They knew that he was in the habit of going to Sabina in Avabäck; she was not particular and received all and sundry. It was at the weekends.

But Nicanor he said: "I'm not so much of a devil that I fuck farmfolk."

And it became a common saying: "He who is a devil, he fucks farmfolk."

It was the horse who kept them alive; Nicanor hauled logs for the firm at Holmsund, and Einar too worked in the timber forest. But the horse made use of everything the poor land gave; besides feed for the horse there were only a couple of stooks of corn; they fed a cow on meadow hay and sedge. The horse was called Gloria. The earth fed Gloria and Gloria fed the firm, and the firm fed them; everything reverts to its origins.

Nicanor was forty-six and Althea was forty-four.

They had taken over their place from one of her mother's brothers. His name was Johan and he was the foreman on a big farm on the coast. He had tuberculosis in his throat; during his last years he could not utter a word; he drank himself to death. Or perhaps it was tuberculosis; he couldn't get a single word out.

Nicanor saw in the papers that the czar of Russia had lost ten thousand horses in the battle of Mukden—they went down into the bottomless swamps, many were drowned in the river Hun, and many more had their legs shot off; the men who survived the battle always carried with them the horses' shrieks of deathly fear and pain. When Nicanor read this he said: "Now at least the czar of Russia will be able to feed his cows."

And then he laughed, the laugh that Althea knew very well, it was only a laugh for the moment, not for life.

In the winter of 1906 the firm bought no forest in those parts, so there was no hauling for Nicanor and no felling for Einar. All they could do was to hunt and prepare wood for their household needs; Gloria had to stand purposeless in her stable like a dummy, though of course she ate. And sometimes in the afternoons when no one needed to see him Nicanor harnessed her, and he said to Althea that a horse could not thrive by standing still, Gloria must have exercise, and trot and pull something; a horse is like a human being, and Althea knew very well that he was going to Sabina in Avabäck.

She was in no way better than Althea; she was listless and thin, she was sort of damp, there was nothing special about lying with her, he had really had greater pleasure from lying with Althea. And he wished that he could tell Althea that: "It is never mostly for fucking that I go to Avabäck. It is not really that I'm willingly unfaithful, but rather that I'm in despair, desperation gnaws at my flesh and consumes my bones; my nakedness would frighten you. You would try to comfort me, Althea.

"But Sabina in Avabäck, she can stand it."

He used to hide his head in her armpit. And then he wept. And she never asked: "Why are you crying, Nicanor?"

No never. She was like the earth he lived on and the world he lived in; it was exactly as if she was asleep.

"I can't achieve anything," he said with his face in against her wrinkled skin. "Nothing ever gets better. Down, everything only goes downhill. All that I do is in vain, everything I have tried has come to nothing.

"I had a go at growing oats in the little fields, but it froze.

"I wanted to go to Holmsund and get a job at the sawmill, but Althea said: 'Never.'

"I wanted to buy a new sleigh on credit, but the shop-keeper, Norberg, said as Althea had done: 'Never.'

"I tried to join a team of log drivers, but they wouldn't have me. I offered them Einar, but no.

"And I read the Scriptures and tried to convert myself, but I'm no good at it. Not like the Lundmarks of Lakaberg or the Burvalls of Storholmträsk.

"And I've taken Gloria seven times to the stallion, Johan Olof's stallion who has as much seed as the sons of Noah, but she is crazy, she is barren, Gloria.

"And now I can feel that pain is on the way, I can feel it at night, the pain is like a frost inside my skeleton; all timber haulers get pain in the end; my whole life is like dragging a sleigh uphill over ice like glass."

And she said nothing. He thought that his thin face, his pointed nose, his spearlike chin, and his sharp cheekbones perhaps cut into her and hurt her sensitive skin, so he turned his head a trifle, then he continued:

"Nothing is left for me. Or will be left by me. Money and food and life just run through my fingers. I never have before me an öre, a seed of corn, a foal, a spoonful of porridge, a bit of meat, or a piece of cake. This is like living without anything before you, it is intolerable, it is like a punishment. A human being must have something before him.

"Oh, to have something before him!"

And Sabina, she lay quite quietly, she breathed slowly as if she slept, as if she had great riches before her.

"And my children," he said. "I have nothing for them. They are as empty-handed as the holy ones in Jerusalem, and empty-handed will they remain, they will have to sell themselves for a pittance. We have given them life, I and Althea, and life is bad and meaningless for those who are bound hand and foot, it simply runs through their fingers. There are those who have control over their lives, those who have bit and bridle and reins, those who have harnessed life.

"But to be enslaved by their life!"

And she was not moved.

"If you knew the sort of life I have lived, Sabina. There in Hundberget. Up on Avaliden. And there in Barsjöheden. And inside Granträsket. Everywhere. Sometimes I have been almost frozen to death. And my load has fallen on top of me. And I've got stuck in deep snow. And frost has covered me in timbermen's huts. And I have been without food for days on end. When life is so bad and hard the meaning must be that man is to achieve something, that there should be something over, that he shall have something before him; one doesn't live just for fun, my life can't be lived just for fun."

And he was silent for a while, as if he thought that Sabina might have something to say to him. But then he said:

"He has trampled me in excrement and valued me as equal to dust and ashes. And what have I to comfort myself with? A horse, Gloria. The firm at Holmsund. Althea."

"You mustn't demand too much for yourself, Nicanor," Sabina then said.

And later she said:

"You'd better be going now, Nicanor. Gloria is standing out in the snow getting cold. And Althea is waiting for you."

But he lay where he was for a while and thought, he tried to think out still more things he could say to Sabina in Avabäck, things that he couldn't say to Althea, but he could not manage it, only the same old words came and they proved nothing.

And Gloria. Gloria was standing outside in the cold wind and might catch the strangles.

On Christmas day Sabina in Avabäck died, it was a stroke. Someone had provided her with schnapps, Konrad in Lakaberg. They found her out by the well. She had just got up the bucket and it had fallen over and the water had spilled all over her and immediately frozen so that she was, as it were, packed in by smooth ice. It was horrible to look at, but all the same in some way beautiful, like a huge jewel, said Ansgarius in Lillåbäck; it was he who found her.

What was he now to do on Boxing Day?

When the holiday was over Nicanor slaughtered Gloria. They heard the shot, and then he came in and said to Einar that he needed help.

And they hoisted her up there to the beams of the portal of the barn, and they skinned her and cut her into pieces. The blood—he poured that out behind the little smithy where he used to bury the dogs. But her head—he could not bear to see Gloria's head. Einar had to lay that in a box for lump sugar and carry it to the forest. "Carry it up to Ormberg," said Nicanor, "and cover it with stones so that the foxes . . ."

Then they helped one another to carry the pieces of meat into the big trough, and it was like meat from three cows. And

Althea thought of the most pitiful women of Jerusalem who had to boil their own children; and she thought of Nicanor's lusts and desires and Sabina in Avabäck, and that he was an adulterer; and it was hard for her to look at the meat. The meat. And she boiled the thighs and hind parts and put them into salty water and what was left she laid in coarse salt and placed everything out in the storehouse.

After that they had food for the whole winter and far into the spring; Althea had to cook her both long and well and she was still tough and tasted of resin; but Nicanor and Einar were of course not at work so they had nothing over, nothing to put before them; and it was as if it were quiet there at the Nicanors; they no longer talked to each other. It wasn't just that simple with Gloria, at once to mourn her and eat her up.

In April he was five days at timber rafting out on the ice, just enough to give him the feel of being out at work again. "I'm as stiff and clumsy as a hay pole," he said. "I feel as if I were seventy." And he had pain in his legs.

"Now there is nothing more left for our Lord but just our bodies, and our stomachs cleave to the earth."

And he thought, But of course the old words that we have in our minds, those we have also. Though the words, the words are almost only air.

And Althea was glad in a way that he nevertheless tried to talk to her.

And Althea could not forget Gloria, she felt that Gloria was alive. She had had a confidante, not to say a sister, in Gloria.

At the time that Nicanor was still out in the forest and came home again for the weekend, the first thing she said was always: "How is Gloria?"

Now she said: "What shall we betake ourselves to without the horse?"

But Nicanor did not answer. And Althea thought, No, I mustn't talk to him about Gloria.

Althea had a miscarriage in May: it was probably the seventh month and it would have been a girl; Nicanor buried her there behind the little smithy, he had made a wooden box for her and put wood fiber in it.

"An unsaved soul," said Althea.

"I don't know about that," said Nicanor. "She is more saved than most people for she is saved from life."

One day at the beginning of June, it was a Saturday and the eldest child was going to Åmträsk to a dance, Althea had found bird-cherry in bloom down by the stream and brought in a twig of it; and Agnes, the smallest girl, had been given a bit of pressing paper and had borrowed the scissors to cut out a doll from it. When Nicanor stood up by the table, he was holding on to the back of a chair, and he wasn't looking at any one of them in particular, it was as if he was looking at all of them at once, and he said:

"Now I can't stand anymore. Now I give up."

They stopped dead and were quite silent and quiet, all the children and Althea. Agnes stopped the scissors and Einar put down the shoes he was greasing and Paulina stood by the stove with the curling tongs in her hand quite still, and tears came into Althea's eyes, they saw and understood that now he was in earnest, he could not stand anymore, he gave up.

"And inside my bones it was like a burning fire so that I could hardly endure the pain and was nearly undone."

After a bit he sat down again, but his face was white and what was said was said.

And they went on doing all the things they had been occupied with, really they had no desire left, but life mustn't stop, must it, just because a man has given up all uncertainty and all hope, it happens every day. It was five kilometers' walk to Amträsk for the dance; and Agnes wanted to get the paper doll finished before she went to bed; and Althea had to take out the slop pail, they had washed themselves; and Victor, the boy who was seventeen, he had to move the buttons on Einar's old breeches so that he could wear them at the dance; and Paulina had to make her hair look pretty. Yes, they all had something they had to do, something important and pressing, but their hands could not free themselves from the words Nicanor had spoken.

And later while they were dancing in Amträsk, both waltz and schottische, and polka, and while they sweated and stamped, and counted the beats, they heard within them: "Now I can't stand anymore, now I give up." The words had, as it were, taken root in their minds and filled their hearts and their blood. And Agnes slept restlessly that night, she heard those words in her sleep, and in the morning she had broken her doll by lying on it; and Althea lay awake, it was as if she were seeking a hole or a slit in this thing Nicanor had said, a gate between the words.

But Nicanor, he at length slept the whole night through without even having to get up to pee.

"Now I can't stand any more. Now I give up."

They didn't know it, but this thing Nicanor had said was like a charge of dynamite, like a gale and cold water when it splits and splinters hot stone. You could not escape those words of his, it was necessary that they should be said, they were devastating, every one of them in Nicanor's house was wounded. Within six months they were scattered before the winds of heaven:

Einar went to Bure and in time became a sawmill hand.

Edna took a job as a maid in Noret. Or perhaps it was Sillarliden.

And Paulina was in the family way and had to get married in a hurry.

Elvina got a wasting sickness and died. It was an internal disease.

Victor made his way to Umeå and became a soldier.

And a couple in Avafors, they were called Nordström, took charge of Agnes. When she was newborn they had said that if things went to pieces for the Nicanors they would very willingly have Agnes, the smallest girl; they were childless.

And Nicanor made it known that he wanted to be rid of the place, the place he had taken over from Johan who had tuberculosis in his throat, and in August they actually managed to sell it to an old couple from Lakaberg, a brother of Konrad's. He had been a tailor, and "every man who has abandoned his house shall get a hundredfold back," said Nicanor.

And so in the autumn they went to America. They challenged America with Nicanor's words. Nicanor and Althea, and they didn't have anything besides what they stood up in, they had shared out the little they had among the children, into the bargain they had sold their wedding rings.

The ship they traveled with was called the *Sabina,* and Nicanor said that that name, it was probably a good omen.

"Though for me she would have gladly been called something else," said Althea. "Whatever you like—*Gloria.*"

Merab's Beauty

THIS you shall know, all created things are unfathomable.

We all have the same spirit, yet most remarkable of all are the cows. No other living things are so filled with spirit and life, their udder that is weighed down by its sap and fruitfulness, and their bellies which compass four stomachs, and within all four there is life; and their eyes that understand and forgive almost everything; and their hides that tremble with happiness. Cows, they have been clothed with spiritual power.

So it was not to be wondered at that he grew despairing when his cows were not left in peace, but came back from the forest with their rumps slashed to pieces.

Gabriel Israelsson was then fifty. He was an old bachelor and had inherited the place after Konrad his father. He had never had any brothers and sisters. He was sort of dried up and solitary—even as a child he was a weakling, and he lost his teeth before he was thirty. He turned his toes out and was a hunchback, and he had unnaturally long arms and his neck was long and crooked and sat, as it were, in front of his chest.

But his cows, all four of them, they were as beautiful and plump as cherubs, they were the most thriving cows in Lakaberg, they were called Merab, Michal, Tahpanes, Bashemath.

And people said that Gabriel Israelsson had unnatural relations with his cows, that he loved them too extravagantly, but it was not true. Sometimes in the winter, though, he slept with them—cows are like ovens and chimney walls: it is as if they had a delightful shimmering glow inside them. And he talked to them and told them what it said in the papers, and it happened sometimes that he told them about his life, and wept about it with them, for what was he to do? This was especially so with Merab. With Merab in particular.

But no one can maintain that this was unnatural.

Once he had had to slaughter a cow called Rizpah—she had broken both her front legs in the big ditch over by Gransjöväg. And no one who was not related or was a stranger was allowed to touch her. He flayed her and cut her up and salted and preserved her in glass bottles. Then he took everything, all that was Rizpah, and went to the parson at Norsjö.

"Cows are not holy to us," said the parson. "They are so among heathens in the land of India."

"But all the same," said Gabriel.

So that time the parson had to give way. And after all it was a whole cow.

The first time that Bashemath came home from the forest in the evening with a stiff rump because she had a blow on the top vertebra of her tail, Gabriel thought it must be some inanimate object that was the cause, a branch from a tree or a stake that had fallen on her.

Or perhaps an unknown cow who had ridden her.

But later when the same happened with Michal, he saw and understood what had happened, that it was a human being and not some dead object, that it was pure iniquity and ill will.

But what can a poor, solitary fellow do against man's wickedness?

For two days he kept them shut up in the cowshed and

gave them last year's hay. But they thought only of the sweet grass around the cool spring over by Lidmyran; it was July and they were furious and mooed continuously. And their stiff tail ends were full of muck, they could not lift them as they usually did, and Gabriel had to wash them with soapy water.

"If only I knew who it was," he said. "Who can outrage life in this way? I'd give him a going-over with my sheath knife, I'd cut him up, he has no right to live."

But on the first day he let them out again it was Tahpanes who got her rump slashed.

And while he washed her and rubbed her dry with a sackcloth towel he thought, It is someone who has no feeling for the dignity of life. Someone whose heart is blind. But Merab he shall not touch. Not Merab.

So the next day in the morning he took his fowling piece and followed the cows into the forest: they walked before him rocking from side to side; here and there they rested by some tussock. Merab went last, she was heavy with confidence and the joy of life, the muscles under her skin moved like waves of water and her udder swayed like a hanging cradle, her beauty was almost like a pain inside him.

Merciful God! thought Gabriel.

He had a bit of smoked meat in his pocket, and when Merab, Michal, Tahpanes, and Bashemath stood still in some good place, he sat himself on a stone and cut himself strips of meat.

Merab's back and sides were black, her cheeks were white and up on her thighs she had stars, white stars, and her ears had white edges and between her eyes there was a light-colored tuft; she was the most beautiful cow he had ever seen.

Beyond Lidmyran, this side of the cool spring, Quaking-Grass Spring, they stopped for the day; first they ate, then they lay down and ruminated, after that they ate again, they did not guzzle, but grazed thoughtfully and heartily; Gabriel sat in the shade under that big pine tree you know, at the back of the spring up in the forest; sometimes he cut off a bit of meat, three times he went to drink—smoked meat is salty.

When evening began to fall they stationed themselves at the edge of the bog and looked toward Lakaberg—Merab and Michal and Tahpanes and Bashemath. They ruminated and thought about the homeward journey; they thought through the paths and coppices and the charcoal burners' sites they had to cross, and the big ditch before Gransjöväg.

And then they began to walk; it was the best part of an hour's way. Bashemath went first and Gabriel reflected that he must buy her a bell, a brass bell, she was in essence a bell cow, she had in her the spirit of wisdom.

But she was no beauty like Merab.

He walked fifty paces behind them; in his right hand he carried his fowling piece. He saw that the berries would soon be ripe. Now on their homeward journey the cows did not indulge in any rests spent eating a tuft of grass for fun; they walked calmly and wisely in a file as if bound together by a rope. Today they will be left in peace, he thought. Today I have saved Merab from having her rump slashed to pieces.

Though that was something he should not have thought.

There by the charcoal burners' sites, the charcoal areas where Erik Granström usually had his charcoal stacks, just when Bashemath had got so far that she only had cinders under her hooves, just at that moment a man stepped out from behind the charcoal burners' hut, the little black hut that Granström had always had there, and he had a spruce stake in his hand.

And Gabriel saw straightaway who it was, he recognized him immediately, he could not avoid instantly seeing and knowing who it was, he ought to have been able to work out long before who it was.

He was a big fellow and thickset and his belly hung over

his belt; he had a sunburned, shining red face, and he was wearing black trousers and a striped gray waistcoat which he had always worn, and the little finger of his right hand was missing—that finger had been cut off when he and a man from Lycksele had fought with lifting pikes at the timber floating. That missing little finger was something Gabriel remembered better than any other fingers God had made.

And he gazed at the cows, he only had eyes for the cows. Gabriel he did not see.

Now even Merab had reached the cinders, she was swishing her tail to drive away the mosquitoes. She was full of food and absentminded and unmilked.

Then he lifted up that spruce stake as if it had been an ax or a leaching club and ran toward her, toward Merab. He said nothing, but his mouth was wide open as if he were trying to shout but couldn't. He was possessed and mad; he aimed with the spruce stake at Merab's rump. Oh, merciful Lord!

Gabriel did not touch his gun, it hung in his right hand, but what use was it? Now that he had seen who it was.

But just when the spruce stake had reached its highest point, just when it had begun to fall toward Merab, toward her rump, he at last came to himself. He drew the deepest breath of which he was capable and tensed his throat so that it was as still as a stovepipe and he yelled, yelled so that it could certainly be heard over the whole of Lakaberg, yes even over in Mörken:

"Old Dad! Old Dad! Don't!"

And his father stopped in the middle of a step and in the middle of a blow and stood still as he usually had done when things didn't go as he had intended. And Merab behaved as if nothing had happened, she wanted to get home to Lakaberg, she was unmilked.

It is no use shooting at a ghost who walks again.

Or to talk to it?

For a long time they stood staring at each other, they kept watch on each other like two bull calves; how can anyone find his enemy and let him escape? And the cows went on their way and could no longer be seen between the trees.

He looked just as he had done when alive, plump, not to say bloated, his eyes were flecked with red, his trouser legs were tight over his thighs, and his hands were broad and hairy; in his nostrils he had hairs and on the hairs hung drops of water.

They had in fact never been able to talk to each other.

But at last Gabriel said: "So, old Dad, you're haunting us, are you?"

But Konrad did not answer.

And now Gabriel recalled what had happened when he died, how he had parted from life.

He had been lying on the maidservant in her bed—they kept a maid at that time—in his right hand he held his gold watch and he had crushed it, whether from lust or from a stroke it was impossible to say. He had the stroke as he lay on the girl, and with his left hand he had dug into her breast, so that they had to bandage her afterward.

"Signe, the maid you lay with, she now lives with Zadrak in Nyklinten," said Gabriel. "They have two children."

Then his face twitched, old Dad's face; it looked as if that pricked him, but he did not say anything.

"You are quite like yourself," Gabriel said. "You haven't changed."

And then at last Konrad opened his mouth. "That is probably true," he said. "The only difference is that I am not alive."

"Though you haunt instead," said Gabriel.

"Yes," said Konrad. "But that is a weak, futile comfort."

He has forgotten the cows, thought Gabriel. I must get him to think of something else. It's a matter of finding the right words, those that are as slippery as butter, words that are like deep water; the cows have still a long way to go. Words, though, had never been his strong point. Even if he felt he had them inside him, he could never get them out.

"Have you ever found out why you are haunting in this way?" he said at last.

"No human being knows why he is alive," said Konrad. "And no ghost knows why he walks either."

If Bashemath had had a bell, a brass bell, then he would have been able to hear how far they had got, then he would have known when they were far enough off, when they stood still by the gate, the bell would have remained silent.

"Is it because of the evil in you that you can't be at peace?" he said.

"I wasn't more evil than others," said Konrad, and he sounded cocksure as he had always done.

"Evil tasted delightful in your mouth," said Gabriel.

"It was the taste of life I wanted to have in my mouth," said Konrad.

"You beat us children," said Gabriel. "With the cane Grandfather left you. And you killed the kittens with your fingers because it gave you pleasure. You stole bundles of wood from Anton's Hanna. You lay with the maidservants though they were unwilling. You always wanted to have six cows though you only had hay for five. Your evil cunning made you always deadly enemies with your neighbors, and you said time after time that you would kill shoemaker Dalin, so that he lived in fear all his life. And you shut Mother up in the little chamber in the loft so that she went more or less mad."

"The maids were willing enough," said Konrad. "And I shut Mother up so that I could be sure of keeping her."

And he pursed his lips and chewed, as it were, so that the muscles in front of his ears moved in and out; and Gabriel recognized that too.

" 'He who purses his lips, he bringeth evil to pass,' " said Gabriel.

That was from the Book of Proverbs.

But then Konrad said: " 'Cursed be he who curses his father.' "

That was the Book of Deuteronomy.

Then Gabriel lost his temper and he said: "I ought to have killed you. I ought to have killed you while you were still alive."

"You weren't man enough for that," said Konrad. And he looked contemptuously at Gabriel, his son. He was thin and crookedly built, he looked like a post and like dried fish. "If you used both your hands you could not straighten out my forefinger," said Konrad.

"Evil has no limits," said Gabriel. "But it is not infinite," he added.

"What you call evil is simply life itself," said Konrad. "That to which you give the name evil, that is what is quite natural."

And what answer could Gabriel give to that? He would have needed the word that was the only right one, he had to search for it, that was what he was searching for all the time. And he thought, Is there a word that is so strong and corrosive that it dissolves those who haunt?

And Konrad said: "It is this hunger. It is as if I have never been able to eat enough."

"You were never a moderate eater in the matter of life," said Gabriel. "But now you are no longer in the flesh, old Dad."

"That's what is so damnable," said Konrad. "I long to be back in the flesh."

And when he said this his face twitched again as if he had a pain inside him.

"The senses of the flesh are death," said Gabriel.

"No," said Konrad. "Life, that is to have a sense of the flesh."

Now they will soon be home, thought Gabriel. Now Merab, Tahpanes, Michal, and Bashemath are safe this time. And he began to cross the charcoal-burning site on his way home.

"You have never understood the flesh," said Konrad, who was walking a few steps behind Gabriel. "You have never understood how to take advantage of the joys of the flesh."

Gabriel wouldn't dispute that, the joys of the flesh. How is one to know what the joys of the flesh are, or what Joy is?

"Is it the joys of the flesh that make you unable to leave the cows in peace?" he said.

Konrad didn't answer immediately; they were walking through the dwarf birch scrub down by Gårdmyran; there were unripe cloudberries.

At last he said: "I can't bear to look at them. And yet I can't let be, they tempt me with some unknown power. I hate them. And they are so well formed and handsome that I could weep when I see them."

"Yes," said Gabriel. "He who knows how to behold a cow, he does not need to look at anything else in the world. He need never have thirsty eyes again."

"Yes," said Konrad. "It is unreasonable that living creatures should be allowed to be as perfect as they are. It is intolerable."

"Their hair is like silk," said Gabriel. "If I knew what silk was like. And their udders are like women's breasts, but more mighty, and they never go dry. And their heads are so full of thoughts that they bow low with every step they take. And their tails move like butterflies, no human beings have an ornament like that."

"Yes," said Konrad. "The tail is probably the worst."

"On the day of judgment cows will be placed on the right

77

hand of the Lord," said Gabriel. "But you will be standing on the left hand among the goats. The cows, they are like God's daughters."

"They are so full of life," said Konrad. "The very sap of life, and it makes me furious when I see them."

"And then you feel obliged to hit them?"

"Yes. Then I am forced to hit them."

"Over their rumps?"

"Yes, over their rumps."

And Gabriel was still seeking for the right word. When he happened to see a ripe cloudberry he bent down, picked and ate it, and he thought, *He* can't do that. He can't eat cloudberries.

"And so it is a sort of jealousy," he said.

"Because they bear the beauty of life."

"Yes," said Konrad. "It is like jealousy."

Perhaps it was that the right word did not exist? Perhaps the right word against the misery of death, its need and its anguish, was not a word of the sort that the mouth can utter?

And yet he was all the same almost like a living being, was old Dad.

And they kept something like company together.

"It's frightfully hard luck on you, Dad, old man," he said.

And when they had nearly reached the big ditch before Gransjöväg, Gabriel said: "You mustn't chastise life. You mustn't hit at it with spruce stakes. You must hold it dear."

And when they got up to the ditch he said the last words just as he was jumping over Gransjöväg ditch, so that he blew a number of words over the ditch out into the air as he jumped, and it sounded as if these words were greater than the others, and the greatest was compassion.

"Love manifests itself only for those who feel compassion for everything in life. Compassion and love, they are what shields us from eternal death."

And he heard the old man, old Dad, take a run at the ditch behind him, and he heard him stamp and jump, and make the leap. But he never landed.

Only the spruce stake was left, and Gabriel picked it up and took it home for firewood.

Perhaps he had in the end found the right word? Though which it was he was never able to decide. He had said so many words, so horribly many. But perhaps this about the cows being God's daughters.

They stood there by the gate mooing, Merab and Michal, and Tahpanes, and Bashemath. And he could hear quite clearly which voice was Merab's.

And when he had milked them and when he had fed them only a little evening supper and watered them, he was up half the night in the smithy, he hammered out a sort of shield out of plate metal, an iron guard to fix firmly to Merab's lumbar regions and her topmost tail vertebra; for all created things are imponderable and you can never be too sure, and no human words last forever. They lose their power.

And toward morning he lay down to sleep for a while beside Merab. She lay ruminating the grass she had found there at the Quaking-Grass Spring, and inside her belly it sounded as it does in the forest in spring, buds and melted snow and weather as of yore.

"Can you understand?" he said to her. "My old Dad. That old dead Dad. All the same, can you understand it?"

Two Letters

Water

TO the County Council at Umeå.

There is water that is cold and dense as stone, you cannot drink it, and there is water which is so thin and weak that it does not help if you drink it, and there is water that shudders when you drink it so that you get the shivers; and there is water that is bitter and tastes of sweat; and some water is, as it were, dead, water spiders sink down through it as if it were air. Indeed water is like the sand on the shores of the sea, its numbers are countless.

So that the form which you, the County Council, have sent us to enable us to tell you what our water situation is, that is useless, there isn't room for water in two lines. If you have lived for seventy years as I have done, then you will know so much about water that the whole County Council could drown in that knowledge.

So I cannot say everything.

When we moved up here to Kläppmyrliden we bought the place from Isaac Grundström; they had six children and thought it was too cramped. Theresa and I had of course no children, we had been married more than five years. Isaac Grundström was going to move to Bjurträsk and begin work at the sawmill—that was when we were cheated over water.

We were here in March and viewed the house, and we asked: "What about water?"

"Yes," Isaac Grundström said, "we have always had water."

And they went with us out to the well—the path was covered with snow—it was behind the cowshed; and he sent the bucket down, it was pretty deep, twenty-five feet he said, and we could hear the bucket hitting water, and at that he jerked the chain so that the bucket filled and then he wound it up, and there was clear water, though perhaps a trifle yellow. And I took the scoop and tasted it.

"Yes," I said, "though it has a smoky smell. And tastes of air. It can't be denied that it reminds one of water from melted snow."

And then he took the scoop and drank.

"It tastes of rock," he said. "You can tell that it is water from a well."

"Yes," I said. "Or water that has pushed up through the ice."

"No," he said. "Water from a well."

Though why should we quarrel about water, there was after all water, so I said:

"Water never tastes the same to two people."

"No one has ever complained about the water here in Kläppmyrliden," he said.

"This thing about water is a sort of habit," I said. "When you have drunk a certain water for a time, then your body is full of that water. And after that you can no longer tell its taste."

So we bought Kläppmyrliden.

But the first winter we lived here, about Candlemas it was, the well was dry.

And we asked people, the neighbors: "How can it be that the well is empty? When we were here last year to look at the

place, then there was water. And Isaac Grundström said that
it never ran dry."

"That well, that runs dry every winter," said the neighbors. "And some dry summers."

And into the bargain they said: "That was why Isaac
Grundström moved. It was because of the water."

"Though last year there was water," I said.

"Never," they then said. "But Isaac Grundström knew
that you would ask: 'What about water?' So they filled up the
well ready for when you came; they melted snow in the
washtub, they worked for three days with the water, they
carried it in buckets out to the well, Isaac and Agela and all
the six children."

"So they filled the well with melted snow?" I said.

"Yes."

"That's how we were cheated."

Though in fact I understood him, Isaac Grundström, he
would not have been able to sell Kläppmyrliden if he had said:
"The only trouble is that the well runs dry every February";
and of course he had to get the place sold.

But things went well for us; we were only two, me and
Theresa.

I tried at first with the cold well at Kläpp, it was only
a few kilometers up in the forest, and I thought, We can very
well carry the water, and I hacked and bored down through
the ice, but the ice ended in moraine earth, it was frozen solid
to the bottom.

After that there was nothing for it but to carry snow and
melt it in the washtub. It was a trifle yellow and had a sort
of smoky smell and tasted of air.

And I said: "Come the summer I shall dig that well a few
feet deeper."

And that's what I did. In May we got our water back,
before midsummer we bailed the well dry and I nailed together

a twenty-five-foot ladder so that I could get down and then I dug, I dug down two feet for sure and Theresa helped me by winding up what I dug loose, it was hard-packed earth consisting of sand, clay, and gravel, and water came, so much so that it was nearly impossible to dig. And I said: "Now we shall never need to be without water again."

And that year we managed right up to the first Sunday in Lent. But then it dried up. After that we had to melt snow until Holy Week when the water came up through the ice.

Otherwise it was good water, the water that was in the well, smooth and clear, though a trifle sweet.

And when summer came again I dug once more.

It wasn't particularly hard to dig, an iron bar and a spade was all I needed. And things were just the same now as in the previous summer, it ran so that I was standing in water the whole time, though Theresa bailed me out bit by bit.

But after that I came down to rock, real primitive rock; I'd only dug down a foot. And I thought, That's the end now. But I might as well dig it clean, I'll clear the rock so that the bottom of the well is like a sitting-room floor, and I dug with my hands so that not a fistful of sand or clay should remain, but as I did it the rock felt like ice to my hands. So there must be a hole somewhere, just like the cracks you find in sea ice. I had the bad luck to open that crack so that the water I had around my feet ran away, the well was dry in a moment, it even sounded as if the rock was sucking up the water, the noise it made was the same as you make when you pull a cork from a bottle, and not even as much as dew was left.

But Theresa said: "It's not your fault. When it's a matter of depth no one can know what it is just right to dig."

After that we were entirely without. And I had not time to dig anymore that summer.

Summer is as short as a shooting star.

That winter we took water from the cold spring at Kläpp,

and when the frost got into the ground then we melted snow in the cauldron that was used for the big wash.

I made a yoke for Theresa so that she could carry two buckets. I formed it to fit her shoulders and neck so that it should not cause her unnecessary pain and produce sores, and Theresa said it was a blessing, that yoke.

If only we had had children they could have carried water.

But neither of us said anything about that. We were unable to have children; the yoke of barrenness is hard to bear. It was hardest for Theresa.

When summer came again I dug over by the woodshed. Theresa stood and pulled up the buckets of earth; I dug down eighteen feet, when I was down to the rock, but there was not a drop of water, the moraine earth was not even damp.

And I said to Theresa: "This damned hump. This dry heap of gravel, this is like the Desert of Sin."

"Though the Scriptures speak of the 'springs of great depth,' " said Theresa.

"Yes," I said. "But how to find them."

"Yes," she said. " 'The springs of great depth, they are hidden,' it also says that in the Scriptures."

"It will be the death of me, this water," I said.

"It isn't the water," Theresa then said, "it is quite the other way around."

"But when summer comes I shall dig again," I said, "then I shall dig a bit below the old well, there must be water there."

"Yes," said Theresa. "For water is sure to be somewhere. It's only hidden like the good wine at the wedding in Cana."

And there was water, an absurd amount of water. I began to dig the first week in June and by the third day we could not bail any longer. Theresa was quite done in, I had got straight down to a vein of water, it was in sand and we said: "Now we shall have water for at least as long as we live, this well will never dry up. So at least there'll be water."

And it was only ten feet deep.

But water must be given time to clear, there is always sediment when it is newly dug, sludge and mud and earth. "The well must be given a couple of days, but then we shall never be without water," we said. "And we will thank Our Lord for this single thing that we have at last been given water."

Though of course we had a trial tasting.

And we said: "No, it still has too much of an earthy taste."

But after a week had gone by it was still not clear, it was yellowish brown and on the surface it shimmered like a rainbow, and we were obliged to say: "No, it doesn't taste of earth, it tastes of iron . . . though it will do for the animals," we said.

But not even the cows could bring themselves to drink it, they seemed to be alarmed and bellowed loudly and flung their heads about when we put it out for them, so there was nothing for it but to fill in the new well and I had not time to dig anymore that summer; and I remember that we had got a stillborn calf, and I put him in the bottom and then filled it in; what good has a man for all his toil, it was nothing but a sort of grave mound over the calf.

That winter we thought, At last! Theresa was certain in October; she was sick and couldn't bear any food but salt pork, and I said it was like a miracle—it was like when Moses struck the rock with his staff. We were anxious, and we rejoiced, it was even so that I helped her to carry water, though the neighbors said: "Oh indeed, since when has it been a man's job to carry water?"

But in December she had a miscarriage, she was carrying

snow down to the washtub and it seemed as if something burst behind in her back.

She recovered quickly, though; she has always been strong, has Theresa, if I hadn't had Theresa I don't know. And it wasn't anyone's fault, how could anything be anyone's fault?

Then in the winter, in February, I heard someone mention a well digger in Strycksele who was called Johan Lidström, he usually went about with his rod and he never made a mistake, and when he had pointed out the place, he dug, and if there wasn't water he would never take any money.

So I sent a sort of message with Andreas Lundmark—he was going to Strycksele in any case when he went to Vindel—and I sent my greetings to that man Lidström and told him that we were not quite satisfied with the water up at Kläppmyrliden, and that we certainly should not say no to his help if he thought he had time.

On the Monday after Whitsun he came. He was tall and thin and had a bit of a hump—perhaps it was the digging—and he was deplorably cocksure and pretty nearly arrogant, he seemed to be a sort of water doctor.

I told him what had happened to us in the matter of water.

"Now we've been living here for seven years," I said. "Without water. And I really have dug. I've dug so that I've more or less got a hump on my back."

I wanted us to understand each other.

"You have only dug haphazardly," he said. "You've fumbled like a blind man in the dark."

"Not so," I said. "I've dug as wisely as any man. You can see for yourself all the places where I've tried to dig."

"Water is strange," he said. "It is inscrutable. It is a sort of science."

"True," I said. "And one can't live without it."

"Ordinary people should never have a go like this with water," he said. "Those who haven't got the right insight."

"When one is without water then one digs in desperation," I said.

"It's never worthwhile to dig in desperation," he said. "Water does not bother itself about people who cry and complain. You can't take water by surprise."

"But you may come right to a vein of water. Like a trick of fate."

"Yes," he said. "And that's almost the worst of it. Veins of water are as touchy as a child's eye. Veins of water are as fragile as a mirage. People simply destroy veins of water when they dig."

"But you, you never make a mistake," I said. "For you things never go wrong over water."

"Never," he said. "I've learned to take water seriously. Streams of water in the earth, they are like the veins of blood in the human body."

And he added: "The King and Parliament should write a law about water. To prevent people digging just anyhow. And they say the world goes forward! I am convinced," he said, "I am convinced that sooner or later they will be obliged to write such a law. Digging a well, that is like putting a child into the world. Life and water, they are one and the same thing."

And he really took pains, he spent a lot of time, for two days he walked about first spying out the land. He examined the grass, he lifted up the turf and smelled the earth, he went about with his rod—it was of fresh birch—and he crept about on all fours and felt his way with his fingers and he lay down on his stomach and kept quite still, he said he could sometimes hear the water bubbling in the ground, he jabbed with his iron pole and pushed pieces of wood down into the holes. He wanted us to see how remarkable it was, this business with water, that it was knowledge and art.

At last, on the morning of the third day, he said:

"This is the place, it is here I shall dig."

It was behind the woodshed, where the raspberries are, it is mostly only gravel there.

"Twenty feet," he said. "Twenty feet, but then you will have water for the whole of your life, and the children and descendants you have unto the third and fourth generation."

"I will do the roughest digging," I said. "Just the top bit. Before we get down to the water itself. I don't want to injure the vein," I said.

"No," he said, "I shall dig all of it. It is the beginning of a thing that decides the end."

And indeed he was a capable well digger. He did not move fast but all the same he was clever. I sat myself down in the barn doorway and mended the rakes, and in between whiles I took a turn and stood beside him, it was as if he sank into the ground, a foot an hour.

And when he got down so far that only his head was visible I took the pail and helped him to heave up the earth, little by little; he was very careful about the corners and he dug square, not round.

And I said to him: "I have always dug round wells. Not square."

"Yes," he said. "I know. People dig round wells. They believe that you must dig them round."

We had to get up a couple of stones with the stump grubber. And I said to him that it was a lucky thing they were not firmly stuck in the soil.

"I knew that," he said. "I never dig where there are stones stuck fast in the soil."

When Saturday evening came, he had dug seventeen feet. He had a thing like a plummet to measure the depth.

"By Monday," he said, "by Monday then we shall come to water. Then you will see a stream."

He was there over the whole of Sunday, he kept close to the well, but he did not dig, he walked about half kicking the earth, and now and then he sat on the mound of earth, he sat and thought.

But Theresa, she said to me on Sunday evening: "Do you think he'll find water?"

"Yes," I said. "He seems so sure."

"I don't believe he'll ever find a vein," said Theresa. "He is too insolent. He's nothing but arrogance."

"If you've hunted up as much water as he has done, you have the right to be arrogant," I said.

"I believe that the man who can find water, he must be humble," said Theresa. "He must have something like love."

And I remembered how I had dug for all those years and found not a drop.

"You mustn't be superstitious," I said. "Either there is water or there isn't. And I believe in him."

At dinnertime on Monday, he had dug twenty feet and I called and asked: "Do you see any water, Lidström?"

"Not quite yet," he answered. "It may be I am short by a few inches."

But when we had eaten and came out again and he climbed down, why it was just as dry at the bottom as when we went in.

And he called to me. "I'll take out a few spits more."

And he continued to dig.

If by chance the County Council really want to know what has happened to us in the matter of water.

* * *

When he had dug twenty-five feet—that was on Tuesday, I wrote it down in the calendar—then I called down to him for the first time: "I don't believe there's water in this place."

But he called back: "I'm quite sure there's water. And I won't give up."

So there was nothing for it but to stand there and take the buckets he filled down in the well; and I felt it with my hand and there was only dry gravel in them. And Theresa came out and stood beside me and I said to her: "It's dry gravel, nothing else."

And then she said: "It's almost worse for this man Lidström. You and I can manage, we are not spoiled in the matter of water. But I don't think he can endure this disgrace."

"So you believe him," I said. "You believe that he has never in his life been mistaken in the matter of water?"

"Yes," she said. "I believe him. Poor man."

"He need not have been so dead sure and so big for his boots," I said. "Even if he usually has luck about water."

"We must think of some way to comfort him," said Theresa. "Kidney-blood pudding. I'll go and cook some kidney-blood pudding."

"Yes," said I. "For he'll never get any money for this dry well."

And I was having to nail new rungs to the ladder all the time.

He didn't eat kidney-blood pudding. He couldn't endure the smell, he said.

When he had got down thirty-five feet, I asked him: "Won't you soon be down to the rock?"

But he answered: "There are ten feet left before I get down to the rock. And on top of the rock there will be water."

But all the same it seemed as if he was a trifle melancholy, when we ate and when we drank our coffee he said never a word, and he went to bed immediately after our evening porridge; he slept up in the attic.

On Thursday morning, though, just as he was about to climb down into the well again, he said: "This is serious. There are those who dig wells, as it were, at random. But for me it is a serious business."

And you could see that this was the truth.

But when I could see by the lead line that it was now forty-two feet, I called down to him: "Lidström, this is absolutely futile. Now you must stop."

But he answered, and it was difficult to hear him, forty-two feet is deep down in a well: "Only a few inches more. Or a foot. Then there will be water."

But I called: "You deceive yourself. You deceive yourself. This patch is as dry as the Desert of Sin."

But he called back to me: "Don't be so deadly obstinate, just go on pulling up the buckets."

And I said: "I don't give a damn for this well anymore. Devil take this well."

But then he called: "Who is it who really knows about water? Is it you or I?"

And when he jerked the chain to show that the bucket was full, I pulled it up. One foot more, I thought. But after that it's finished, after that he must climb up the ladder himself with his buckets of gravel.

And on Saturday morning—we were just going to have our midmorning coffee—it was forty-five feet.

"Lidström," I shouted. "Lidström. Not an inch more. Not even a grain of gravel."

But he answered: "Don't you interfere in this. I shall dig as deep as I please."

And I shouted: "You have promised to dig two more wells in Norsjö this summer."

"Yes," he answered. "But I only dig one at a time."

"But I have other things to do than to stand here heaving up buckets," I said. "I haven't got the summer left."

"When there is water," he shouted, "you'll be grateful that I didn't give up just because it was a few inches deeper than one thought."

And I could hear even up there how he continued to dig and delve as we were talking.

"But Lidström," I shouted, "don't you understand what I'm saying to you? Now there must be an end to this. Now you must come up. This is the end of the dig."

And then he called from the bottom of the hole where he was, which was perhaps the deepest well in the Norsjö district:

"You can't order me about. I shall dig as much as I please. I have my freedom. I am a free human being. And a free human being digs as long as he pleases."

And it seemed as if I had no patience left. I felt I was forced to get him out, even if I had to climb down and carry him up the ladder myself.

"But the land is mine," I screamed. "The land you're digging down into. I shall decide myself if some stranger comes here and digs deep dry holes. No outsider shall try to take command over this stony ground."

And I stamped on the ground, I was so provoked, I stamped hard with my right foot on the ground.

And then there was a rumbling down in the well, it sounded like rain on a barn roof, it was the south wall of the well that gave way, it wasn't strutted, and I hastily jumped backward a few paces; the edge above the well was moving too, there was no moisture to hold the gravel and sandy soil together so it rushed and ran like the sand in an hourglass; it was like it is when powder snow fills in a footprint in winter; the whole well disappeared as if it had been dug down in a large lake that had again fallen back into place, all that was left

of the well was a sort of hollow in the ground, that forty-five-
foot well.

And I was powerless, wasn't I?

And I called to Theresa and she came out and we stood
there a while, she had tears in her eyes and she said: "Think
if he had to suffer."

"It went so horribly quickly," I said. "I even believe that
he is still standing upright. He is standing upright at a depth
of forty-five feet."

"He wanted to do his best," she said. "That was all he
wanted. To do his best."

"I told him to come up," I said. "If he had done as I told
him, this would never have happened."

"Yes," she said. "He was pigheaded. But perhaps they are
like that. Well diggers."

And I was obliged to betake myself to Norsjö. I wasn't
quite sure how to proceed.

"He is standing upright at a depth of forty-five feet," I
said to the parson. "It would take me the whole summer to
dig him out again."

And the parson, he turned the matter over in his mind for
a bit, then he said: "At sea one commits a dead man to his
eternal rest right on the spot. Those who lose their life at sea,
they are not fished up from the depths to be sunk into conse-
crated ground. This well digger Lidström, the man who is
standing upright at a depth of forty-five feet, he is like a sailor
who has drowned in his ocean."

So I returned home and shoveled back the earth into that
hollow. I put back everything that Lidström had dug out, hard
packed earth and dry gravel, so that it looked smooth and tidy
again, and I planted some raspberry bushes there, and Theresa
made a wreath out of rowan twigs, and when two weeks had
passed the parson came and carried out the burial service, yes,
it was called burial service, he said when I asked if it was really

necessary to say: "From earth thou comest, to earth shall thou return." And he had been told by the parson in Vindel that this Lidström had no family nor any kinsfolk in Strycksele, he was a recluse of sorts, and the parson read the verse about water from Matthew: "And whosoever shall give to drink unto one of these little ones a cup of cold water, he shall in no wise lose his reward."

And Theresa said to the parson, "He assured me that he had dug over a hundred."

Nevertheless we were still without water.

And I said to Theresa many times: "If there was only one person who did not mind about water, then we would sell Kläppmyrliden to that person. But we are stuck with Kläppmyrliden."

But Theresa, she said that we only need take one day at a time, we only need carry as much water from Kläppkallkällan or melt as much snow in the washtub as we need for the day. And we are only two, aren't we?

"We are only we two."

But I said: "Think of our old age, Theresa. Who will then carry water for us? And melt snow?"

And she had to admit that I was right.

So I went on digging in various places, though I knew it was in vain. I dug down into the dry gravel and the moraine earth; it was as if I felt obliged to dig a dry hole every summer. Dry gravel is like a colander for water, it's like a sieve and a tub without a bottom.

Our neighbors all had water. In Lakaberg and Inreliden and Böle and Avabäck and Åmträsk, yes even where they had water, people keep a sharp eye on those who haven't got water. And we were a childless couple who didn't have water, so that . . .

We were like Kläppmyrliden.

And Kläppmyrliden, it was like the Desert of Sin. Life, too, has an incurable drought.

After fifteen years had passed since the summer Lidström was with us—yes, that's what we said, though he was actually with us still—the fifteen summers, so to say, it was an unbearably dry summer and I was standing down by the small spruces of the barn sharpening the hay poles. Then Theresa came out of the house carrying the coffee basket, she had a bonnet on her head and was wearing a big apron, her baking apron.

And we were no longer young, I was fifty-eight and she was fifty-seven.

I wouldn't tell everyone this. But I will tell the County Council the truth. Since the County Council have asked about water.

And we didn't have intercourse any longer, that intercourse that man and wife usually have, we hadn't strength left for everything, and dragging ourselves along up at Kläppmyrliden had taken it out of us. And besides it was in a way futile.

We sat down on the grass, she had baked a sponge cake and she had brought out a jug of fresh water and I drank the water and looked at her and saw how wrinkled she was and how gray-haired, and that her cheekbones were much sharper than they had been and that her shoulders were a bit crooked and that she had a lump of the back of her neck, it was the yoke. And I thought, Perhaps I should take time off and make a new one for her, one that lies like a shawl around her neck.

And it was as if she heard my thoughts for she said: "I've been thinking about the water. Whether we have been too zealous about water. So that the water has tied itself into a knot. If we hadn't searched for water so desperately, we might perhaps have found enough and to spare."

She has always been superstitious about water, has Theresa.

But I did not say that. I did not say that to her, I just moved a bit closer and put my right arm around her, for this thing about water has always been a sort of sorrow for us; and she leaned her head against me, and we lay down there on the grass, and then we tried to do what we hadn't done for years, it was, as it were, unplanned.

It was an inspiration.

And then after a bit I was obliged to say: "It doesn't come for me. I can't manage anymore."

But then Theresa said: "That doesn't matter. There is so terribly much one can never finish. I only wanted you to taste the sponge cake."

Her patience is like a blessing.

And then she said: "I've got wet behind, on my back."

And I said: "It's not possible. It is as dry here as in the Desert of Sin."

"Feel me, then," she said, and sat up.

And I felt with my hand. And she was as wet as if it had rained.

"You should have a try at digging in this place," she said.

"No," I said. "I'm sure I've dug in this place ten times."

"But if I beg you to," she said.

So I was obliged to fetch the spade, and she stood and watched while I dug, and I dug just where she had lain in the grass, and the grass was shining as if it was dewy, and the water came almost immediately. I had not dug as much as two feet and there was a jet of water as big as a fist, and it spilled over the edges, it was a real spring.

Yes, that's how it's been in the matter of water. It is a good spring, not sweet and not bitter, it does not taste of ice water or of rock, and I've built a frame around it, like a wall around a well, and I shall finish it this summer, and I shall make a lid.

It does not freeze to the bottom in winter so I can answer you like this and tell the County Council that we have water, we have water till our dying day, and we shall leave water behind us, and it is called Theresa's Spring.

True Love

Hällmäs Sanatorium
25th August 1941

Dear Brother

Now I'll sit down to write to you. I have the afternoon before
me, you must forgive me if my letter is a long one; you know
how unpredictable I am. That your letters are as short as
glimpses of the sun in winter I can well understand, you have
strong lungs and no fever and so you have neither rest nor
peace. You have your fever too in your own way.

My patches and glands have not changed.

Elna and Agda are dead. And Arne away at Bränntjärn—
it's a month ago now—he was thought to be getting better,
he had had an operation on his ribs and had no doubt that he
would be sent home in the autumn. But it flared up, it flared
up, and now I must tell you what happened, since I was
perhaps not entirely without blame; it flared up and after a
week he was gone. He had an easy time of it, though he had
dreaded it so much. He was thirty-one.

You remember what he was like. Small and fair-haired
and easygoing; he played the guitar.

He was keeping company with Vendla, she is only

twenty-three and born in Vindelgransele. She is related to the Lindbloms of Ristjöln; she is slender and has a terribly lovely face, she wears her hair in a big bun on her head, she has a strong nose and big lips; she is a believer.

Arne was too. A believer.

Arne and Vendla were fond of going for walks in the forest. Vendla had two patches on her left lung, but she had got better even since she came here; she says herself that she does not feel a thing, only that perhaps she is a little hotter than usual. Hotter! They are in the habit of going for their walks in the forest after dinner, and usually sit down and rest behind the topmost clump of spruce trees.

And I had seen that, had seen how they sat there twining their fingers together.

And one day toward the end of July—it was a Sunday and hot, burning hot, though I was only wearing a short-sleeved shirt the sweat was pouring from me as if I'd been in a timber forest—a Sunday it was, when I followed them.

They walked more quickly than I did, and he had his arm around her; she was only wearing a blouse and skirt, and it was a skirt that was, as it were, slit at the side. I was in no hurry either, one must reserve one's energies and only use those that can give one pleasure. The harebells had come out, and I took an oxeye daisy and put it in my shirt pocket.

When I arrived at the topmost point of their forest walk they had already sat down. I could see that Arne was almost annoyed that I had not left them in peace, Vendla moved a comb she had in her hair. She had a bag of chocolates.

But I sat down and we began to talk about the war. I can remember to this day exactly how things were; the spruce gave off the smell of hot sunshine, there were ants in the grass and Arne was wearing a blue silk scarf around his neck under his shirt.

"They'll be taking Russia now," said Arne. "Though what can they want the whole of Siberia for?"

And I said that they probably did not know, they weren't taking Russia in order to use it for anything in particular.

"But if you take something, you can no doubt find some way of using it that gives you pleasure," I said.

"First you help yourself, then you satisfy yourself."

"Hitler is the Beast," said Arne. "He has broken loose and the whole world looks upon him with amazement. He has got the power to wage war and subdue peoples and all the inhabitants of the world must worship him."

And Vendla said nothing. But I said that it could well be that Hitler was the Beast.

He had read about it in the Book of Revelations at night, he said. He had not been able to sleep. "Fire shall fall from heaven upon the earth and all those who do not worship the Beast shall be killed and peoples shall be led away into captivity, and the Beast is scarlet."

"Hitler's color is brown," I said.

"But he is scarlet inside," said Arne.

We were half sitting on the grass, a real Sabbath peace reigned; I stretched myself out so that I got a trifle nearer Vendla; you know my long legs and my long stooping back and my hands that I like to have free before me when I talk.

"And he'll soon fall upon us," said Arne. "Sweden will be drowned in blood."

And Vendla, she said nothing, it was as if she was not listening; she had hitched her skirt up a bit over her knees; now and then she helped herself to a chocolate.

"So you think Hitler may concern himself with us. What would he want Sweden for?"

Then he sat silent for a while and thought.

"But surely you can see," he said and pointed to the forest and the hills and the Vindel River.

"Who would not want such a land?" he said.

And it was probably true.

I warned you at the start that I should be writing a long letter. Now you can see.

"But he won't affect us," I said. "What use would a sanatorium be to him?"

And to that Arne had at first nothing to say.

"He will shun us like the plague," I said.

But then Arne said: "We shall be butchered like all the rest."

And then I understood that he was really to be pitied. But what could I do?

"Hitler will butcher us, he won't make any distinction between us," he said.

"You are afraid," I said. "You are really frightened."

"Yes," he said. "I am terribly frightened. And it's worst at night."

And he told me that Vendla had said it was the same for her, though now she sat not saying a word; I'm not even sure that she was listening. She said nothing. You remember that I've always been upset by frightened people. Frightened people, they alarm me.

"Of what should we be afraid?" I said. "We who live on a knife edge."

"A knife edge?" he said.

"With this illness," I said. "Our lives can be cut short. At any time. So why should we be afraid?"

"So you mean that if one has consumption one need not fear Hitler?" he said.

That was a difficult question to answer, so I had to think for a while.

"First one accustoms oneself to fear," I tried saying. "You accept it as you accept the taste of a water you have to drink every day. And then you break the habit of calling it fear. And then it is transformed into a sort of hope."

Though that was not really what I meant. I had wanted to say it much better, particularly because Vendla was listening. She had lain down on her back and had a stalk of grass in her mouth.

"So that fear and hope should be, as it were, the same thing," said Arne, and you could hear that he thought I had got myself into deep waters and that he thought he had got the better of me.

"If one is afraid then one just grabs at rescue all the time," I said. "Like a man who is drowning, as if there were nothing but rescue at which one could grab. And one never has time to grab life itself."

And then I said this which I never should have said: "I celebrate marriage with life each day."

Those were words that Arne couldn't bear to hear, they were too strong for him, they hit home like a blow from a hammer, he began to cough and after that he spoke not a word more to us that day.

But Vendla, she sat up abruptly and looked at me, and it was as if she now really looked at me for the first time. I celebrate marriage with life every day, and small wrinkles appeared around her eyes and she opened her mouth slightly and moved her lips a bit as if she was repeating what I said to herself, and she was incredibly beautiful.

After a little while we got up and began to go down the hill. We said nothing more for a long time, and Vendla walked between us, but now she walked a bit nearer to me, a sort of gap seemed to have developed between her and Arne. Arne had suddenly begun to cough a bit, but we walked along kicking stones and bending down to pull up stalks of grass with our fingers and to look up at the clouds and to try to pretend that there was nothing amiss. The heat was closer and more oppressive now, though we were going downhill. And now and then I felt Vendla's hip against mine, it was as if she bumped against me with her buttocks gently and carefully but with determination. I celebrate marriage with life every day, and I could feel how the muscles in her side rolled and heaved as she walked.

And when we were halfway Vendla said, and I remember it word for word just as she said it: "I am not frightened as I really might be, not because I am a believer. Not for the sake of eternal life. But because I know that everything is temporary and will pass. Even that in which one believes is only there instead of something else."

And she went on: "You yourself choose what you will believe in and be afraid of and hope for: What one should really believe, that is beyond our reach. Even belief is temporary. So why should one be afraid all the time?" she said.

That is just what she said, word for word.

And when she said that, I felt that she was the wisest human being I had ever met.

Everything is temporary and will pass, and that which is really something in which one should believe, that is beyond reach, therefore people need not be as frightened as they could in fact be.

When we got back to the sanatorium Arne went straight to his room and lay down. He had already understood how things were. His cough got progressively worse, he remained in bed.

That is what has been a torment to me all the time, I should never have said those words, if one lives on a knife edge you can be infected by a few words: I celebrate marriage with life every day.

* * *

That evening I stole into Vendla's room, I got there without anyone seeing me; and she let me in immediately, it was as if she were expecting me.

We hardly talked at all, it was not necessary, for we had already said most of it, but we stood for a long time with our arms around one another, as if we had lived apart for an unbearably long time and at last met again; she rocked backward and forward as if one of us needed comforting.

The whole thing was so obvious. And when she undid her bun it seemed to me almost as if she opened her whole self to me, her hair was like the Virgin Mary's headcloth in a painting. Her room faces west so that she had the sunlight over her; and we were both so excited that we became breathless and were slightly aware of our coughs; true love is short and flickering.

But for Arne things went quickly. During the next few days he had several minor hemorrhages and he did not leave his room anymore. We were not told anything, Vendla and I, here one is never told anything.

Vendla has a sister in Avaträsk, they are said to be so alike that one cannot tell one from the other. She runs the café there and belongs to the choir in the mission house. You can go there and see her. Then you will know.

But on the last day of Arne's life I was allowed in to see him; one is not usually allowed. There wasn't much left of him, you know how it is. And he wanted me to read to him.

It was the First Epistle of John. "Herein is our love made perfect, that we may have boldness in the day of judgment because as he is, so are we in this world. There is no fear in love; but perfect love casteth out fear; because fear hath torment. He that feareth is not made perfect in love." And later that night he died.

* * *

I have wanted to tell you about this; you knew Arne in Bränntjärn, and sometimes I feel I have some sort of responsibility for things going as they did; I should never have said what I did about what I do with life every day.

But it is most probable that he had had a cavity for a long time.

I must end now, it is suppertime and I want to send this off at once, I don't want this to lie about, that haunting anxiety will never leave me and Vendla. She is waiting for me up in the hall.

I hope that life is strong and good for you each day, and that you will hold out.

Greetings to everyone. Your loving brother

The Stump Grubber

I T is an implement.
I tell you this so that you may understand that it is not a human being or a monster, neither is it only wood, and bits of iron and cable and hook.

Three large sturdy legs made of wooden posts and on top the pulley, and then the cogwheels, it is the cogwheels and the pulley that do all the work, and on its side a winch of iron, and you put the cable around what is to be lifted, a stone or a stump, and you fasten the cable with the hook, and then you wind the winch around, and for each turn you make with the winch you lift the stone or the stump a fraction of an inch, your strength is multiplied a thousandfold. With a stump grubber a poor weak creature can raise slaughtered horses and stones that are fast in the ground.

He needs help, though, to carry the stump grubber and put it in place.

But if you lose your grip and if you have not locked the winch with the ratchet, then the object you have lifted falls back and all the power returns to the winch and that power is converted into speed and it whirls around so quickly that you cannot see it, and it crushes without mercy everything that comes in its way. Then the winch is like the hand of God's wrath.

Jacob Lundmark and Gerda, Jacob's Gerda, they lived on the smallholding Inreliden. They had bought the partition in 1918. He had himself sawn the wood for the house and built it, and he had cleared and cultivated two fields so that they fed a cow; in the winter he was out in the timber forest, and in summer he hewed charcoal wood for the farmers. He had built the cowshed out of old timber that he had bought from Eric Markström in Bök. He was not a big stout man, Jacob, but tough and muscular; his nose had been crooked since his childhood, he had been kicked while helping to shoe a horse.

That was when he was ten, his job was to hold up the back legs, he stood just behind the horse. Then his mother, Alfrida, came out and saw him standing there—he was the apple of her eye—and she shouted to the men: "No, Jacob mustn't lift the hooves, it's dangerous."

And he abruptly straightened up to say that he was indeed not too small to give the blacksmith a hand, and the horse didn't like that and ever since then his nose had been crooked and he had a red mark just under his right eye.

Gerda, she was from Örträsk, so she didn't know anyone and no one knew anything about her for certain, so she was on her own. The only person she talked to occasionally was Isabella, Isabella Stenlund, the woman who had the illegitimate son. But that was only a few times a year. On the wall she had a hanging, it was one of the corduroy hangings, a blue one, and it said on it:

THE MYSTERY OF FAITH
IN A PURE CONSCIENCE

It was probably taken from the First Epistle of Timothy. She was plump but not fat.

Between the house and the cowshed at Inreliden Jacob had left a pine tree, a huge pine which he thought could be a kind of good luck tree; he had spared it. No one could embrace it, though many had tried, not even Nylundius the preacher, though he could embrace seven feet; and the forester Nicolin had said that it might well be the largest pine in the Norsjö and even in the area of Lycksele he did not know of a bigger one.

But Gerda was of the opinion that the big pine was, as it were, gloomy and depressing and that it kept out the light, she liked light, she delighted in it, so at last Jacob took it down and had it sawn up, and out of it he made a bed, a big wide bed, and a gate-legged table and six folding chairs, and a door for the small room—before they'd only had a piece of drapery there. That was in 1924, and their third girl Dagny, she was two years old.

But the stump was left.

And even the stump was enormous. A district forester came all the way from Ruskträsk just to see it, and to measure it and count its rings, and he said that the big pine had been like Methuselah, its days were like those of the sand.

And Jacob said that that stump was too much for him, its roots went out into the Vindel River to the south and out into the Skellefte River in the north, the big pine had certainly drunk from two rivers at the same time.

But to Gerda the stump was hateful, a human being sees what he has an eye for. It was in the way, she wanted to plant currant bushes there, or they could put in raspberries. Isabella could give them the plants, it was somehow a savage and ungodly thing on their farm where she wanted everything to be smooth and neat; it was a graven image.

So she said: "Dearest love, Jacob, can't you get rid of that stump?"

"I don't know whether I'm equal to it," said Jacob.

"You can burn it up, or bury it, or prize it loose with a crowbar. It makes me feel ill, it is hateful and nasty."

"A stump like that has superhuman strength," said Jacob. "An ordinary human being was never meant to fight with a primitive monster like that."

But in the summer Jacob got hold of a ghastly stump grubber, it was up for sale at the auction of the effects of Elis of Lillåberg; the legs were twenty feet long, it was the stump grubber they had had when they made the Ajaur road. He got it cheap, it was a sort of monstrosity and a show-off, almost impossible to use—big men like Elis of Lillåberg don't exist these days. Jacob got it home on an open-sided wagon, as he had already borrowed Gabriel Israelsson's horse and was going in the direction of Svartliden.

By the last Saturday in July he had got in the hay and then he set the stump grubber beside the stump of the great pine.

And he thought, Men walk upon the earth like trees. And those who serve not He will tear out by their roots.

He exposed the thickest roots with a spade and with his ax he chopped off everything that he could get at for the moment, and then he dug deeper and took his pickax and even an iron bar; and he chopped and prized loose so that he could remove the small stones and the moraine soil with his fingers; when the bark was cracked a smell of turpentine came from the stump; the earth smelled too; and he hewed off the tough roots with his ax, and it didn't worry him that it struck sparks out of the gravel and became blunt; it was for Gerda's sake he was doing this, and once he had started upon the stump there was no question of turning back and no mercy, he couldn't worry over the bluntness of his big ax, he could grind it on Monday.

* * *

He was dripping with sweat and he had to take off his blue smock, but he always sweated horribly when he became eager and was putting his back into it, and the gravel tore his cuticles and his knuckles so that they bled, but he took no notice; the roots were as thick as the thighbone of a horse and were just as many as the boughs had been on the pine itself while it was still alive; and when he stuck his crowbar down into the ground he continually struck new roots that went in all directions in the depths; and he began to imagine that it was the pine that had held together his whole plot with its roots, and that if he were finally able to lift the stump the whole of Inreliden would crash together and be scattered; and when he dug and heaved and lifted the roots with his crowbar, then he was aware that there was still life in that stump, the roots bent a trifle but only enough to make their strength and toughness apparent; and he said to that stump that, true enough, you are terrific, but a man too is tough and he has muscles and he can work out one thing and another that are beyond your powers of understanding, and moreover he has his stump grubber.

At last he was forced to straighten up and go in to Gerda and drink some water.

"Aren't you going to take a rest soon?" she said. "It is Saturday after all."

"I'm only working on that stump," he said, "only by way of passing the time."

Then he went out and carried on.

When the time came for them to eat their evening porridge she came out and called him; he only ate one plate of barley-meal porridge. And she asked if she should not wash the small wounds on his knuckles and if he would not pull off his dirty clothes and put on his new trousers and his light-colored shirt. It was after all the weekend, and the children wanted them to sing together and to read stories from the fairy-tale book.

But he heard from her voice that she had only one thing in her mind, that was the stump.

"It isn't really any sort of work," he said. "This job with the stump, I'm only trying to feel my way, and to reckon how I can best get it out."

He looked at her, her downy arms, her round chin, the little dimples in her cheeks, the gray-blue eyes that were sorrowful and happy at the same time—they were like some sort of warm spring—and on her forehead the little wrinkle that the parson had said meant deep thoughts.

And he suddenly felt almost happy to think that he might still be lucky enough to raise the stump and that when morning came she would be able to come out and view the big hole in the ground.

The earth was harder and harder the deeper he dug; the pebbles and gravel and clay were packed together so that they were almost like boulders, and he couldn't understand how the roots had penetrated them down in the depths, they might even have eaten their way into the rock; it was as if the pine had decided to stand forever and ever.

But at last the largest roots were dug loose and chopped off and free.

Then he fetched the stump grubber. He lifted first one leg then another, only a few feet at a time: if he hurried, the stump grubber might get the upper hand and crash down—besides he had the whole night. He stood aside a few paces to see whether he had got it into the right position, and when he saw that the cogwheel and pulley were right over the stump, he stamped it fast into the ground with his feet and his iron post.

Then he took the steel cable and pushed it in under the stump, under the roots that he could get at, and pulled it up in several places, under the worst of the thick roots, and finally fastened it firmly in place with the hook, the big iron hook, so that there could be no mistake, nothing could come loose, and the weight would be evenly balanced so that nothing could go wrong; now it was, as it were, an even contest between him and the stump.

And he sat down there on the grass and looked at the cable and the pulley and the winch and the stump grubber. And the stump.

Now, he thought. Now.

And he thought, Gerda is standing behind the curtain watching me.

And he asked himself this too: What is she thinking? He had never been certain of what she was thinking—though no human being knows what love or hatred in others he has to deal with.

What were they thinking down in Örträsk?

First he wound the winch the number of turns needed to tense the cable, then he stopped to see that it had not gone slack under some root—it is important that the steel cable should always be stretched, that it is straight and that there is not any dislocation or weakness in it—then he made a few more turns so that the cable began to sing, it sounded as the ice on a lake does when it is going to break up.

When you use a stump grubber you must not be in a hurry, you must stop from time to time, there is a ratchet that you can drop down against the cogwheels to which the winch is fastened so that it does not unwind.

Then he made one turn at a time and rested a bit between each turn, it wasn't possible to make more than one turn at a time.

The half turn when the winch is going up is done with the muscles of a man's arms, back, and legs; when the winch goes the half turn down, you lean on it with the upper part of your body and press it down with your weight.

In a little while the small roots began to give way, you

could hear a snap far down in the earth when they broke, and Jacob thought, All the same it is moving, it is not invincible.

That means half a turn at a time; and when the winch is going down one can lean against it and rest for a few breaths.

And he thought, If it were not for the fact that this undertaking is mine, if this hadn't been put solely and only on me, then I would have spoken to Gerda and asked her to come out and help me, by leaning on the winch with the little bit of weight that she has after all.

It was the south side of the stump that gave way first, it snapped so much that at first he thought it was the cable that was being torn apart, but then when he got the winch down he saw that the stump had risen some half inch and that the earth had cracked around the roots where he had not dug and he said: "Dear God, let it give way on the north side too."

But he didn't want to let down the ratchet on the wheel yet, the ratchet of a stump grinder ticks like a clock; if you use the ratchet you can't lift anything silently.

After yet a few more turns only the south side was moving: I shall have to fasten it firm with the ratchet, he thought, and dig and chop a bit on the north side, otherwise it will tilt over. And then I shall have to let it down once more and start again from the beginning. I'll do three turns more, he thought. Only three turns. No more.

Now he had to exert himself to the full. And he could feel how the veins on the outside of his neck were swelling so that they pressed against the neckband of his sweater, and what a strain it was on his thighs and arms so that it was almost like having a cramp, and the red mark under his right eye throbbed, and the winch cut into his palms so they were on the way to being flayed. Perhaps I ought to let down the ratchet, take a rest, and put on my gloves, he thought.

Never before in his life had he exerted himself in this

way. But neither was this work in the ordinary meaning of the word. It wasn't only that he had said: "I shall go at it and get up that stump before I take a rest day, that huge stump." No, he had a quite special sort of obligation and there was no mercy, and there behind the curtain in the living room Gerda was watching him.

For the sake of that a man can give up everything, he thought. For the sake of that a man can forget himself so that he is no longer aware of the blood and sinews of his own body.

And confirmation: then came a snap like a gunshot on the north side and the whole stump shook like an animal wearing a slaughtering mask and the south side sank down a fraction so that the north side should have room to rise.

Gerda, thought Jacob. Gerda.

Now I'll take no more rests, he thought, now I'll not drop the ratchet, now it's a matter of not giving up, now I have the better of it and I won't let it go, even if I have to fight until the morning.

The only question was: would the steel cable hold?

After each turn that he now took roots rose a half inch or so, they split there in the earth and cracked and groaned and broke as if they'd been strands of wool, and the little stones and the earth ran back into the hole, and the little roots that had not broken came up and were peeled; it almost felt as if the stump was giving up and blessed him. And he hardly took a rest when each turn was completed, if he had stopped the pain and ache in his hand might get the better of him; and he thought that no human being had ever pulled such a mighty stump out of the ground, there was almost something solemn about it, and Gerda is standing there and sees how calmly and firmly I wind the winch of the stump grubber.

And very soon the stump hung almost free, it rocked and swayed a trifle on the cable and sometimes it tilted as if in its helplessness it were trying to shake itself loose; it was even larger and more horrible than Jacob had thought, you could clearly see that it was by nature infernal, it was, as it were, shaggy.

And the cable sang like the strings of a violin.

If he could only get it up high enough to be able to lift it to one side with a pole and lay it down on the edge of the hole, then everything would be over, then he'd take a rest, then he would go in to Gerda and say: "I pulled up that stump, I got him up because I had the stump grubber there."

At last there were only two roots holding the stump to the earth, they were half peeled and as stretched and tormented as the sinews of Jacob's body, they trembled as if they'd been alive. They were on the north side.

Jacob thought about his hands, he'd lost all feeling in them; they are benumbed, they are benumbed by pain, he thought, perhaps the skin will fall off them like a pair of gloves; after this is over, and after I've had a rest, then I'll let my hands rest too, then I'll submerge them in cold water, and let them take a holiday and get back their strength, for one's hands are the body's crown.

And just then, just when it was all nearly over, Gerda came out onto the porch—he did not see her as he was standing at the back of the stump—and she was holding Dagny by one hand and in the other she had Dagny's doll, and she called with all the strength she had in her body:

"Dearest love, Jacob! You must be careful!"

And that call, that was the most wonderful thing Jacob had been sensible of in the whole of his life, it was so inexpressibly warm and trembling, and so permeated with concern and love that he halted halfway through the winch, her call had made him quite weak and dazed, he felt that he must see her, and he turned his head and the upper part of his body so that she would perhaps be in sight, but he still held on to the winch, and he could really see her, she was standing on the porch and in her left hand she held the little girl and in her right hand the doll, and the evening sun lit her up from the side so that he could see how her apron clung to her stomach and thighs, and she had bound up her hair with a blue shawl, and her mouth was open, and her eyes were wide open with anxiety and fondness. No human being could seem more heavenly.

And she called to him once more:

"Dearest love, Jacob, you must be careful!"

And just as she called for the second time, he got the feeling back in his hands, and he could feel that they couldn't do any more; his fingers began to straighten themselves out and he could not stop them, it felt as if there was no longer any mercy for them, and he tried to make the half turn that was wanting to bring the winch down to the bottom, but he had not the strength.

And then the last rootlets broke, they gave way suddenly and the stump, which was now hanging free, tipped over and swung around as if it were possessed by a frightful fit of rage, and Jacob was quite helpless, all he could hear was Gerda's voice within him, and the thickest root of the stump gave him a horrible blow on his hip joint, just on the sinews of his hip, a tremendous blow on his hip so that he fell forward and his fingers gave way altogether, and all the strength in the stump went back into the winch. But within him all he saw was Gerda, and he was bursting with her voice and her words, the eagerness and anxiety and warmth, her fondness for him that was so great that there were almost tears in her voice, so that when he fell headlong he did not grasp what it was that was happening, he did not realize what had befallen him. What it was that struck him like the hand of God's wrath and tore his breast open and killed him, if it was the winch, or if it was the almost unbearable heat of love, there are words that are like glowing coals, "Dearest love, Jacob, you must be careful."

Legender

Translated by
Mary Sandbach

Boundaries

THERE were four farms in Korpmyrberget: Enar's, Anton's, Oscar's, and Otto's. Otto's was in the middle, it was surrounded by the other three.

Each farm consisted of 4.942 acres, and along the boundaries square stones had been placed.

Enar and Anton and Oscar were married and had heaps of children; Otto was unmarried and childless; he was thickset and his face was as wrinkled as a workman's glove.

The farm was the only thing close to his heart; he knew his farm as he did his own body—it was dry and barren.

If he had any joy in life it was in his farm, Korpmyrberget 1:1.

So it was not surprising that he should want his farm to grow and be developed; that is what we want to happen with those we love.

He began to move the boundary stones, he did it carefully and in secret and at night, just a few feet; he carried them against his thighs, with bent knees and unsteadily.

If I do it carefully, he thought, then Enar and Anton and Oscar will never notice anything, no one can remember so precisely where the boundaries run, not within a few inches; the earth and universe are remolded continuously but so slowly

and protractedly that we are not aware of it. Bays get clogged
with weeds, streams alter their course, trees fall and rot, mountains sink, and the deeps rise up.

But at last Enar and Anton and Oscar became suspicious.
A heap of stones that Enar had always believed was his suddenly became Otto's. And Anton's path that led down to
Korpmyrtarn now ran through Otto's forest. And a couple of
huge pine trees that Oscar had rejoiced in ever since his childhood had wandered off and one day stood on Otto's ground.

So they consulted among themselves.

What if it were not Otto but someone else?

And if one had known for certain where the boundaries
really ran.

If only Otto were the sort you could talk to.

And if it had been a matter of life and death.

So they agreed to wait and see; it might be that Otto was
suffering from an illness, this moving of the boundary stones,
a sort of impulse.

But when four years had passed Otto began to take their
arable land.

Then they wrote a letter to the Land Surveyor's Board
in Umeå: the boundaries of Korpmyrberget 1:1 must be re-
drawn or staked out anew.

So one day in September the surveyor came; it was to
Otto that he came. In a leather bag he had a surveyor's chain
and a theodolite and pencils and a ruler and other instruments.
He was a calm, quiet surveyor, he wore balloon breeches and
puttees and his hair was parted with a ruler.

He said that two executives from the Land Surveyor's
Office would have to be called, but Otto said there was no
hurry, first of all the surveyor must have a bite to eat.

So Otto made barley-meal porridge and put out milk and
cranberries, and then he sat down on the woodbox and regarded the surveyor. He ate slowly; he did not seem to be

eating because he was hungry, but because it was his duty. He kept his left hand spread out and dead still on the tabletop and he sat straight and still on his chair; he looked like a seven-inch nail, and he did not bend forward when he ate, yet all the same he never spilled anything, and he ate in squares, he made straight edges with his spoon, he had put the porridge in the middle of the plate and he smoothed it and made the corners quite rectangular, and then he ate carefully and exactly as much from each side so that the porridge was all the time a perfect square; even the last spoonful of barley-meal porridge was square.

"You eat in squares," said Otto. "I've never seen that before."

"If you ever for a moment allow disorder into your life," said the surveyor, "then you are lost."

"Are you always so precise with everything you do?" said Otto.

"I am a man with backbone," said the surveyor; "so far I have never taken a step or performed a manipulation by chance."

"It is of course very fortunate," said Otto, "never to be dependent on chance."

"If you give chance a little finger, she will immediately take your whole hand," said the surveyor. "If you take chance in your boat, you will then have to row her to land."

"So you plan to be precise about this business in Korpmyrberget?" said Otto.

"I shall do everything anew," said the surveyor. "I shall stake out every boundary, as it were, from the beginning."

"You certainly seem to know the meaning of your life," said Otto.

"Life is entirely meaningless," said the surveyor. "That is why order is so indispensable."

"I believe," said Otto, "that life has a meaning."

"If life itself had a meaning," said the surveyor, "then no laws or boundaries would be needed."

Then Otto realized that the surveyor was an impossible person. He wanted to bring to an end all those small improvements to the boundaries of his property which it had cost so much toil and so many years to bring about; he was without compassion or mercy. To him one farm was just as sacred as the next.

So that when they got outside Otto went to his woodshed, fetched his ax, and killed him. He was obliged to, the surveyor had just opened that enormous bag. Otto killed him in secret, and then carried him to the dung pit. Getting rid of a surveyor is not all that simple, he buried him a good three feet down.

He carried the bag up to the attic, for you never know—that chain was brass and the bag was ox hide, real shoe leather.

For a time there was of course talk about that surveyor who had disappeared. No one had seen him. They formed a human chain in Björksele and dragged halfway to Korpmyrberget, and the constable went around for a time to the farms and asked if anyone had seen a townsman in balloon breeches, but later on they said that he must certainly have drowned in the Vindel River. Otto did not know anything, he hadn't even been expecting a surveyor. It might also be the case that that surveyor had lost his way and would eventually appear in Ammarnäs or Sorsele.

Soon people had forgotten him.

Anton and Enar and Oscar went to Sikseleberg and stayed there over the winter working the timber forest, and they never once remembered to talk about the surveying of the land.

When spring came Otto moved the muck, he took the largest part of the dung pit to the potato field. He used a bushel; he spread the dung with a pitchfork, and when he prodded the heap with the pitchfork there was nothing that was solid and had not decayed.

The wonderful thing about a dung pit is the way in which it ferments and burns and refines. It is like a charcoal stack where everything is changed but nothing is finally lost.

After that he had to set his potatoes.

No, there was nothing left of the surveyor, not even his boots or puttees or balloon breeches, nor yet his skeleton, including that backbone he had talked of, it was all gone. And Otto was almost pleased that the surveyor in this case had been so obliging and compliant and had disappeared so amicably and meekly. Though when he was nearly at the bottom of the muck pit the cranium got stuck on one of the prongs of the pitchfork.

The acids and the fermentation and the warmth had not bitten into it one bit; it may have been that the surveyor's head had been firmer and more immovable and had denser material in his skull than elsewhere. And Otto put it to one side: it was a large, impressive skull, it would be negligent and wasteful just to throw it away—it is a great sin to let any created thing be destroyed.

Otto always wanted to do his best.

When he had nearly finished setting the potatoes, when he was in the middle of the last row, he went and fetched the skull and put a large potato with many eyes in it just behind the frontal bone. He then put the cranium and the potato in the sunniest row, which was usually the most productive.

That summer he again allowed himself to move a dozen boundary stones; he and his farm mustn't become rigid from anxiety or placidity.

He lifted the potatoes at the end of September. He knelt in order to spare his back.

He had forgotten that he had put one potato in a skull.

Therefore he was in a way astonished when he dug it up.

It was on the second day of the potato lifting, about midday, the potato had bred most supernaturally, the cranium was full of new potatoes, as if a field mouse had made its hiding place in it. The potatoes lay in curved, carefully arranged rows, like logs in a stack or piglets when they are sucking, as the thoughts must once have lain in the surveyor's head.

And Otto knocked the potatoes out of the skull into his cloth cap and carried them in and put them in the larder. The skull was left to dry for a time, then he pounded it into meal, one can't lightly allow growing power like that to be wasted.

Then in the autumn he made two cow necklaces of the surveyor's chain, they looked like necklaces of pure gold.

When he had killed the pig and was going to eat the ears and the tail and the trotters he took out his surveyor potatoes.

After half an hour they were still not cooked.

When he tested them with a fork after an hour it still could not penetrate the peel.

Boiling only seemed to make them harder, the fork rang when after two hours he had another try. Toward evening the water had boiled away, the potatoes lay rattling in the bottom of the pan. The surveyor potatoes had turned into stones. Square stones. They looked like boundary stones.

He put them back in the larder.

And he got himself a maid who declared that she really could boil potatoes. Boiling potatoes is the foundation of all human life.

And she boiled them for fourteen days, the fourteen days she was with him, they seemed to become sort of shiny outside.

He never touched the girl; he did not even bother to look at her, though she undressed in the kitchen in the evenings and stood there just in her underwear.

And in May he set the potatoes again, even the surveyor potatoes. You never can know anything for certain.

During the summer, stones increased on the potato field,

they came up everywhere, a tip and a side here, a flat surface there. They looked like boundary stones.

So he began to pick up and carry. He made a little sleigh on two shafts, a sleigh with a birchbark basket to use for picking up stones. He put the stones on the mound of stones below the woodshed.

In August he built a supporting wall by the shed wall, it was easily done with those square stones; the mound was soon up to the eaves.

The skin of his hands was worn, his back was injured by stone picking, he had horrid pains in his hips and shoulders.

His sleep was affected, it is a disgrace for a man to have stonier land than others.

In September he tried to lift the potatoes. The few he found among the stones were no bigger than a thumbnail, and gave no more than half a barrel. The boundary stones had quite got the upper hand, those square stones that had been created in the surveyor's skull, just behind the frontal bone.

He was obliged to build a new mound behind the flax-drying shed. At night he took the stable lantern, dipped the light, and hung it around his neck by a strap, so that he could see to scrape and pluck up and garner his unnatural harvest.

He tormented himself to such a degree that the blood forced its way up to his mouth. But he never tried to boil a single stone; in fact he never gave himself time to cook any proper food. He ate swedes and turnips raw and hacked pieces off the dried fish.

And the potato field sank and dropped below the surrounding land; the stones that he had moved had eaten and drunk the top soil.

On All Saints' Day he gave up. He gave up and lay quite still for two days on the kitchen sofa. The wall clock never struck for he had given up winding it. He covered his face with two loose pages from the collection of sermons: the First Death and the Judgment.

On the third day he made his way to Malå and went to see the doctor, Doctor Rudvall.

And Otto told him about his back and his hands and his hips and knees and feet. Yes, he gave an account of the whole of his body.

"So could I get a painkiller?" he said.

The doctor examined him.

It was all very simple, a blind man could have seen it: his back was finished, his hands were worn out and his hips were crooked and his knees destroyed by pain and his feet done for.

Then the doctor asked how so much misery and deficiency had accumulated in one body.

Then Otto told him how things were, his potato field was infested by stones and he had to rip out this infestation by the roots. Square stones grew like weeds out of the soil, little boundary stones reproduced themselves quite recklessly.

And Dr. Rudvall realized that it was the stones and the potato field that were the illness.

In the evening they went together to Korpmyrberget; it was night by the time they got there. Otto's whole body was in pieces and he wanted to go to bed, but the doctor simply had to see these stones that belonged to the vegetable kingdom.

So Otto fetched the lantern—there was a hoarfrost—and he bent down and picked up a surveyor stone and shone a light on it.

And the doctor stood for a long time and peered, and he twisted his head this way and that as if he wanted to view the stone from all sides.

Then he said: "I can't see anything."

"Don't you see the stone?" said Otto.

"No," said the doctor, "I can't see the stone."

Then Otto lifted the lantern still nearer, he held it an inch from his hand and said: "But don't you see?"

But Dr. Rudvall said: "No. I can only see your empty hand."

Then Otto held his hand in front of his eyes, and suddenly even he saw that the palm was empty.

"I must have dropped the stone," he said.

And he picked up another stone, he took hold of it with all his five fingers and gripped it as hard as he could and held it out to the doctor.

"What about this?" he said.

But again the doctor said: "No, I can't for the life of me see any stone."

And then Otto could feel that his fingers were squeezing empty air and themselves as if they were affected by a cramp, and he said: "It's my hands. They won't do their work as they should."

And he gave the lantern to the doctor and went down on his knees and dug with both hands into the earth; and he saw surveyor stones everywhere, but no sooner did he try to take hold of them than they disappeared, they crumbled to bits and turned into nothing but earth, they were elusive. He crawled here and there over the upper corner of the potato field, he struggled and groped and fumbled and the hoarfrost burned his palms like fire, but he could not capture a single stone. At last he had to stand up and look at the doctor, who stood holding the stable lantern in front of him. It was plain to see that he understood the whole matter: Otto felt as if the doctor saw right through him, nothing could be hidden from Dr. Rudvall, and boundary stones that seem to multiply uncontrollably in a potato field, such a thing never happens to a person by chance.

"I shall never understand life," said Otto.

"Yes," said the doctor. "It is a sort of mystery. Life."

"Can you wait a moment?" said Otto. "I only want to fetch an implement."

So he went to the woodshed—he had no choice—and he fetched his ax that was stuck fast in the wall, then he went back to the doctor and killed him, he killed him secretly and then he dragged him by the feet to his dung pit and buried him. Thereupon he went indoors and went to bed. His whole body was aching so much that he was only half conscious. He fell asleep immediately and slept for forty-eight hours, in spite of the fact that he had not been given a painkiller.

The search for Dr. Rudvall was frenzied, the people of Malå went round Får swamp and Malå swamp to see whether he had floated to the surface; patients sat from morning to night in case by chance . . . the constable went between the villages and single farms asking after him; the river Mal was dragged as far down as Strömfors. The like of Dr. Rudvall they would never be able to get, at least not in Malå—he had been quite like a normal human being, like God's chosen man.

But then on a Sunday came the snow, three feet in six days, and after that it was no use worrying anymore about Dr. Rudvall.

Otto was in a poor way all winter. He looked after his animals, carried in wood, and lit the stove, and that was all he did—no carpentry, nothing in the smithy. It was the first winter that he was without occupation, he who was otherwise so wonderfully clever with his hands.

But the day after Holy Thursday he carted out the dung.

Nothing was left of Dr. Rudvall, his clothes were gone, and his false teeth and his beard and his cranium, he was gone forever. Otto didn't even have him in mind as he scooped out the muck: all the same it was God's blessing that he was so far recovered that he could handle the pitchfork.

But then he got up the hand, it was the doctor's right hand, it was quite fresh and undamaged, it was so steeped and saturated with medicine that it could not possibly decay; the forefinger was outstretched as if there was something that should be pointed out.

When later on Otto set the potatoes he took the doctor's hand and put a potato into it, a fine large kidney potato, and he closed the fingers around it—it would be a shame not to use such an excellent hand—and he set it in the lowest row but one.

It was a summer with night rain and great warmth, a real potato summer.

Otto lifted the potatoes in the last week of September, the frost had already melted down the tops; he had wrapped some sacking around his trouser legs so that he could kneel and dig.

In the last row but one he found the doctor's hand again.

Of the hand itself very little was left, and of the large potato the hand had grasped, nothing but a slimy smear, but round about it were the loveliest new potatoes.

They were large potatoes, yellow, uniform, and smooth-skinned, kidneys, and each potato was fine, they looked like a bony hand with five fingers, even the joints and the nails were visible, this is how the five-finger kidney potatoes arose, they were the most beautiful potatoes Otto had seen in the whole of his life.

There are said to be five-finger kidney potatoes in Storsel-bränna even today, you can get seed potatoes of them there. Otto is said to have given half a bucketful to a cousin who lived there.

Otto tried eating one that very evening and the potato was like the yolk of an egg, and this single potato was nearly a whole meal; the rest he put aside for seed potatoes. They were possibly a trifle difficult to peel around the joints.

* * *

After two years Otto only had one row of ordinary kidney potatoes, the rest were five-fingered ones.

And he got better and more active, his back and his feet healed, and his hips straightened themselves out and his hands and knees recovered, now and then he felt strong enough to move some of the boundary stones toward Enar, Anton, and Oscar; there seemed to be something healing and health-giving about those five-fingered kidney potatoes.

And the surveyor stones were largely gone from the potato field.

When Dr. Rudvall had been gone for three years his nurse married Constable Hultin in Malå; she had given up hope.

That autumn she heard of a man in Lycksele direction who made keyhole mountings that were supernaturally beautiful and well made.

It was Otto who made these keyhole mountings, he made them out of the surveyor's bag that he had put away in the attic.

The nurse and Constable Hultin came to see him on the last Sunday in September; they had left the horse and trap in Svartliden and walked the last mile; and Otto got out the keyhole mountings.

And the nurse asked him how he had managed. She had never before seen such lovely curlicues and delicate curves; no, she had not even been able to imagine them. Otto was truly a divinely inspired artist, his keyhole mountings were, as it were, saturated with beauty and spirituality.

Then Otto produced the punches and pressing forms that he had forged and carved; he grew strangely warm inside when he listened to her; he even brought the press that he had built for the keyhole mountings, it was a gigantic screw clamp with three thick wooden screws.

Even Constable Hultin thought it was an admirable and

wonderful piece of apparatus, and Otto became so excited that he brought out a bit of leather to show how he made those mountings. It hardly ever happened that people talked to him, he actually sweated with eagerness and joy, and while they were standing there talking, she caught sight of a bucket of potatoes that stood half under the table, and she said: "Those are remarkable potatoes."

"They are five-fingered kidney potatoes," said Otto. "I cultivated that sort in a hand I had got hold of," he explained.

Then the nurse picked up a potato and looked at it; she looked especially carefully at what might be called the potato's forefinger.

And quite suddenly she remembered something she had ordered herself to forget.

She had always wanted Dr. Rudvall for her own, and one day in the May of the last year—he was in Malå—she had told him so; she could not do without him, he could do what he liked with her, for her he was the meaning of life, she wanted to belong to him forever.

All he had said was that he was not made in such a way that he wanted her.

That might have meant anything. That evening she bit his forefinger. A man had come from Mörtjärn who had chopped his leg to pieces with an ax, and when the doctor had sewn up his wound, and she had to bite off the thread, she was overcome by a horrid impulse and set her teeth into Dr. Rudvall's forefinger and bit him so hard that afterward she had to help him to sew it up.

And he of course had a deep scar.

It was this scar that she now saw on Otto's five-fingered kidney potatoes. She picked up several potatoes and examined them, and on every one there was this scar.

"It is a curious thing about the human bite," she said; "it

is so hot that it is reproduced throughout creation like the glow through a lump of peat."

And she asked: "In whose hand was it that the parent potato grew?"

And Otto the cultivator, the creator, swelled with pride. "It was Dr. Rudvall's," he said.

Constable Hultin saw immediately what this meant.

Before they set off—now of course they all three went together—she bought six keyhole mountings from Otto.

Otto made a cone of the First Death and then of the Judgment, and put in them twelve five-fingered kidney potatoes, the new sort which were probably the great symbol and meaning in his life.

"You can even eat them raw," he said. "As picnic food."

"Our whole life," he added, "our whole life is one single uninterrupted wonder."

In time one of his sister's sons took over the farm; at nighttime he is in the habit of moving one or other of the boundary stones toward Anton, Enar, and Oscar.

And they let him be, he only moves them a foot at a time; to set about him would be meaningless: he is that sort of person and he can't control himself. In his heart of hearts he is pure and blameless; he is innocent of his impulses; no man creates his own impulses. He is not going to give up until he has moved the last boundary stone to the ends of the earth.

The Weight Lifter

ONE day in May at Åhlen's in Klaraberg Street the Spirit came upon Anette Svensson.

She had bought sausage, carrots, milk, and hard bread. The Spirit came upon her just after she had paid and was swinging the plastic basket containing her goods up off the steel-topped counter in front of the cashier.

Anette Svensson was twenty-one and she lived alone. Earlier on she had tried, as an experiment, living with three different men. She believed it had become clear to her that love was a mystery. It was raining.

Came upon her is what it did—that's what she thought. She also thought, Struck, possessed, penetrated, filled to the brim.

And, in passing, Laughing gas, she thought.

It is true she had never had laughing gas. She only knew it by name, but all the same. The Spirit is a kind of laughing gas.

She had never belonged to any religious sect, she had not even been confirmed. All this came out bit by bit in the police investigation.

Her outlook on life was sometimes dark, sometimes sunny. She lacked an outlook on life.

She did not see the rain and she did not feel it against the skin of her face. She went down the steps to Vasa Street; perhaps the drops in the air about her evaporated because of the heat she had suddenly begun to radiate.

Later on she herself would say that she felt herself filled by a hidden strength; that her feet moved perplexedly and without effort; that she had lost her foothold but neither did she need it; that she had voluntarily, yes ultravoluntarily, delivered herself over to the aforementioned strength; that she had all at once seen through a secret the nature of which she did not understand; that with absolute certainty she knew something that was unknown, unknown to her; that two play-school classes on the way to Drottning Street were lit up by a dazzling but invisible sun.

The rain, of which Anette Svensson was not aware, had made the asphalt slippery, and in Vasa Street twenty meters ahead of her, a pedestrian, an actor from Västerås, was, at that very moment, run over by a taxicab.

Just when the accident happened, just when she heard the dull thud and the screeching tires and the onlookers' frightened yell, just at that very second she had thought, Why must the Spirit also descend upon the innocent?

The actor was crushed tight under the front wheels of the cab; he lay quite still, like a mechanic who had fallen asleep at his work; he kept his mouth half open as if he were searching for a line. A considerable crowd had quickly gathered around him; Anette Svensson heard voices calling out: "He's not breathing! The back of his head is crushed! He is dead! His spine is broken! His chest has been squashed in!"

She particularly noticed a group of women; the taxi driver, who was sitting in his cab frightened and unhappy, was also staring intently at these women. They were holding their hands to their mouths to check their screams; they were all enormously fat—there were only five of them but, with their huge bodies they took up as much space as twenty ordinary people. In their midst stood a tall and very thin man with a sad haggard face and a drooping mustache.

No one made a move to intervene or to fetch help, everyone seemed to regard it as something completed and final. On many faces there shone a look of unusual peace, as if this situation had been the soothing and satisfying goal of a quest that had been going on for a long time, a quest for exactly what was precisely complete and final.

This immorality frightened Anette Svensson; it seemed to her more horrible than the accident itself. And the Spirit in the form of an inner voice said to her: "Get going, Anette Svensson, all release begins with movement!"

Here the writer must temporarily make himself heard above the text. "Can a person really hear inner voices? Are not the occurrences of inner voices a sign of illness and decay, presaging the dissolution and splitting of the personality, a threat to, why even a cancellation of, the existing compact between the self and the world? Should not the healthy man's innermost being be full of silence?"

"Yes," says the writer.

"No," says the text. "Inner voices are quite normal occurrences."

"Our imagination creates inner voices when we are beside ourselves," says the writer. "Spirits and inner voices are the delusions of the devil!"

But the text continues.

All release begins with movement, and Anette Svensson went up to the taxicab, took hold of the front bumper with both hands, and without any real effort lifted up the whole vehicle; now released, the actor came to his senses immediately, got up, and recited the lines from *The Tempest* that he had been so diligently searching for as he lay crushed under the cab: " 'If the devils come one at a time, I could fight my way through legions!' "

The man with the drooping mustaches, the man in the midst of the absurdly overfed women, now rushed up to Anette Svensson. She had calmly and carefully lowered the cab to the street again. He was panting, his voice was shrill but at the same time hoarse, while he talked to her he held her left upper arm in a bony but persuasive grip.

He explained that he was on the way to Toronto. The ladies in his company were the strongest in Sweden, the world championship in weight lifting for ladies was going to be held in Toronto. He demanded that Anette Svensson should immediately join his troupe, indeed he not only demanded: he implored her, he ordered her in the name of God and the National Swedish Athletics Association!

And yet once again she heard the inner voices: "Yes, Anette Svensson, nothing more will happen here, there everything can happen, never Here but There."

The competition was held in Borden Hall, Toronto.

Anette Svensson was weighed and put into the bantamweight class.

The competitors had to lift a bar to whose end heavy metal disks had been attached. They were led to a stage one by one in front of an innumerable public that was muttering and grunting—thousands of people had come to Borden Hall. When the weighted bar had been lifted up into the air in a few fleeting seconds, the public roared with released passion which immediately subsided into a monotonous grumble of disappointment. No release lasts forever.

The leader, he of the drooping mustache, Hemming by name—he had very hastily informed Anette Svensson that this was his name, it embarrassed him as it meant "loose skin," he would much have preferred being called "powerful body"—this leader explained to Anette Svensson that she ought to make her first lift at the beginning of the contest.

"After that you can wait," he said; "when all the others are eliminated, then you go in and lift as many hundred kilos as necessary."

"A Mercedes!" she said. "A Mercedes with driver! That weigh two tons."

All the competing ladies appeared uneasy and excited. They walked about with small tripping, bouncing resilient steps, they pulled and panted, they shook their vast limbs and cried, "Ahoo." But Anette Svensson remained perfectly calm, yes indifferent. And of her indifference she thought, It is the Spirit.

Then her turn came, her name and fatherland were called by a loudspeaker. Hemming offered her ammonia to sniff from a wad of cotton wool and pushed her onto the stage. She smiled at the public; the stockinette dress that Hemming had lent her hung in heavy folds on her body; she had sprinkled her palms with talcum powder.

But she could not budge the weighted bar.

No, it lay immovable in spite of the fact that she tensed her sinews to the bursting point and that she shouted, "Ahoo."

Only a hundred kilos and she could not even make it roll! And within her she heard the Spirit: "One hundred kilos! Too little by half!"

Yes, of course, thought Anette Svensson. What is a hundred kilos to the Spirit?

The public muttered bitterly with disappointment. Anette Svensson resignedly made two more fruitless efforts to lift or at least to shift the weighted bar. Finally she bowed deeply three times and threw five kisses to the public. Through the thin cloth behind the stage she could hear Hemming weeping from disappointment and despair; she too could feel the tears tickling her throat and eyes, and, tottering uncertainly as if her frail body had lifted an unimaginable weight, she retreated backward out of the glare of the footlights. The public did not even bother to whistle or mock her in any other way.

Hemming did not offer to comfort her with an embrace, no, not even to offer her a red-and-white-checked handkerchief. He only groaned: "You are a disgrace to athletics!"

And she did not even manage to get her answer past her lips: "It's all the Spirit's fault!"

No, Anette Svensson crept away into a corner behind the toilets. There she sat while the contest proceeded and was decided, *Ahoo,* she sat motionless on a sandbox with her face pressed against her updrawn knees. She was a disgrace.

"Well, she has only herself to blame," says the writer. "She can very well do so. What the hell was she doing there with her inner voice and her Spirit?"

"Blame herself?" says the text, and raises its voice. "No person can ever blame himself. Don't imagine you can ever write a single line of which the meaning is 'blame yourself'!"

"Anette Svensson is not stupid," says the writer, "but she lacks intellectual discipline. For instance, what did she do with her plastic basket with the sausage?"

"Not even you can blame yourself," says the text.

"Whatever you write you are blameless. And she forgot the plastic bag with the sausage and the carrots on the bus to Arlanda."

When the contests were over Hemming came up to her; the public and the ladies who had competed honestly were leaving Borden Hall; all of them were both satisfied and disappointed in different ways. Anette saw her image reflected in his eyes, a blot.

"You and your Mercedes," he said.

"With my own strength I can do nothing," she said. "I should have mentioned it to you. Everything depends on the Spirit that works in me."

"The Spirit?" he said.

"I don't know him very well," said Anette Svensson. "I have only quite recently had him. I got him at Åhlen's on Klaraberg Street."

"I never buy anything at Åhlen's," said Hemming, chewing his mustache angrily. "I bought a pair of leather gloves there once, and they were plastic. What sort of spirit is it you are talking about?"

"I don't know," said Anette Svensson.

"And what has he to do with weight lifting?"

"The Spirit can lift anything whatever," said Anette Svensson. "That's all I know."

"But not a paltry hundred kilos?" said Hemming, without in any way trying to hide his scorn. He sneered at Anette Svensson and he sneered at the Spirit.

"Just so," said Anette Svensson. "A hundred kilos is too little by half for the Spirit."

"And what would be just right for it?" said Hemming. "Five hundred kilos? A couple of tons?"

"You mustn't blaspheme," said Anette Svensson.

"I don't blaspheme," said Hemming. He had never before heard the word *blaspheme*.

"Four hundred kilos," said Anette Svensson. "The Spirit can't be bothered with lesser weights."

Then Hemming fetched a weighted bar and fastened new weights to its ends; they were now alone in the large room behind the stage. He pulled and groaned, but said not a word, he seemed to have quite forgotten the other ladies in his troupe—at last he fastened the disks with large screws. His movements were jerky and hasty, he was sweating with excitement and rage. At last he said: "Four hundred kilos! Now you can show what you and your spirit are good for!"

"Four hundred kilos! That is more than any human being of whatever conceivable sex you please has ever lifted!"

And Anette Svensson took hold of the weighted bar with both her hands, lifted it, and held it with straight arms above her head. She had no need even to say, "Ahoo," it cost her no effort, she did not tremble, it seemed to her that the bar soared into the air by its own power.

If anyone doubts that this is true and that it really happened, the text will, in a decided, matter-of-fact voice, inform you that the name engraved on the polished steel bar was:

ELEIKO HALMSTAD SWEDEN

And Hemming looked at her. Tears filled his eyes, yes, he really wept from emotion and happy impotence, he believed but his belief made him despair.

When she had again placed the bar on the floor he said: "Anette, you matchless talent, you must learn to lift like an ordinary woman. If you make an effort you will be able to lift a hundred kilos, with great difficulty a hundred and twenty kilos, if you force yourself to the uttermost you will lift a hundred and fifty."

And she said: "Hemming, you don't understand the situation properly."

"What you need is technical training," he said. "I will show you how an ordinary person lifts."

And with a quick movement he removed the six disks from the bar.

"Now!" he said. "Now you will see and learn. Now a new life will begin for you. Now you must watch my legs, my back, and my arms carefully."

He rapidly threw off his clothes; his underpants were adorned with the national coat of arms. And with an *Ahoo* that made his mustache flap like the wings of a bird he lifted the bar, he stamped his feet, the muscles of his arms and legs trembled and throbbed like anxious hearts under his skin, he lifted the bar on lightly bent arms and slightly crooked knees.

When he was about to bring his feet together and move his arms and legs something unexpected happened.

He seemed to be overcome by a moment of giddiness. His eyes squinted as if they were trying to turn inward, he took two stumbling steps forward, his hands and arms were twisted or bent backward so that when he unavoidably fell forward he was hit by the bar that fell with him; it hit him an inch below his shoulder blades, and there he lay.

Anette Svensson saw immediately that something serious had happened: blood was trickling from his nostrils, the bar was crushing his chest, now and then spasms shot through his outstretched hands, his chin and mouth, which were pressed against the floor, were twisted into an apathetic sneering grin. They were alone, the room was only lit by two weak ceiling lights; she looked for a telephone but could not find one. So she did what she had to do: with her left hand she lifted off the bar, she took him in her arms, he weighed little, and she carried him out through a door to the left of the stage EMER-GENCY EXIT, down a narrow spiral staircase, along a long corridor—he was as limp as a rag doll and his skin was sticky with sweat—out through a heavy iron door and into the street.

If only he had not been so horribly strong and so fright-fully weak it would never have happened, she thought and tears collected and made a milk-white pool on his chest. A taxicab stopped and its driver looked long and thoughtfully at Anette Svensson and Hemming, a weeping woman holding a limp naked man in her arms. He recognized it, it was a picture he had seen in his childhood, an old painting or a sculpture, the sight gripped him in a strange way and he drove them to the Hospital of the Virgin Mary.

"Was this absolutely necessary?" asks the writer.

"Yes," answers the text. "Necessary and obvious and unavoidable."

Hemming recovered consciousness after forty-eight hours, she kept watch by his bed. Or more correctly: a third part of himself recovered consciousness. His back was broken, the whole of his splendid body below his fifth rib was sadly useless.

And he said to her: "It's all your fault."

To this naturally enough she had no answer.

For three weeks he remained at the Hospital of the Virgin Mary. After that he was transported home. The Swedish Society of Weight Lifters paid the expenses. Anette Svensson went with him—it was all her fault.

Out over the Atlantic, that terrifying void between sky and sea, he asked her, and he shouted out his question for his stretcher was placed in the tail of the plane close to the engine: "You'll never leave me, will you?"

She didn't want to answer, but all the same there was a piercing, heartrending answer from within her: "Only death can part us!"

Hemming had previously never had a woman, he had only had the gigantic ladies. Now Anette Svensson moved in with him in his little flat in Piper Street. She became his nurse, she trimmed his mustache and boiled his six eggs every morning, she emptied his urine bag when it was full and she washed his wasting body; it was wasting away in spite of all the eggs he ate and in spite of the fact that he believed his bone marrow would grow together again, and every evening she read aloud to him from the evening paper's sports pages and some bits out of the *Guinness Book of Records.*

Yes, you could almost say that her hands carried him through life, *Ahoo.* They were not married, there was no reason for them to be married, she was his woman and he was her invalid, they were united by a bond that was infinitely stronger than any marriage could ever have been: her ineffaceable debt to him. Hemming always called Anette his wife.

Seven years passed and they never asked from whence she got the strength she needed for this ceaseless lifting and carrying, this many-sided heaving and lugging, this awe-inspiring weight lifting. But both were convinced that the strength was called the Spirit, and in their heart of hearts they carried the conviction that the Spirit should be called the Holy.

Sometimes she said to him: "I love you." That too she owed him, it had to be borne. And sometimes he would grasp her hands without any obvious reason, and hold them fast, and only scrutinized them. He wanted to see the Spirit.

And he suggested that they should go out on tour, and that for money she should display her strength, and he reckoned up for her all the things she could lift: blocks of concrete, buses, men piled one on top of the other, drums of oil, ponies. But she said: "You are enough for me."

"I take it we are nearing the end?" says the writer.

"Don't ask me," says the text. "In this instance the lifting and carrying and lugging can go on for an eternity."

"I don't trust you," says the writer. "Above all I don't trust that thing called the Spirit."

"On the contrary!" answers the text. "I truly wish that I was less predictable and that the Spirit was more unpredictable!"

"First you decide the rules of the game!" says the writer. "And then you complain that you must follow them!"

"I would willingly stop here," says the text. Here in the warmth and tenderness of 29 Piper Street, third floor. Anette Svensson was in the habit of carrying him downstairs and up, he constantly wanted to go on trips, to athletic contests, to remarkable sights which in his immobility he was afraid of forgetting, to inns where, in the days of his strength, he had eaten unforgettable portions. But a text may never think of its own convenience, it must drain itself to the bottom and only show its true face at the end.

"I chose between weight lifting and rock climbing," Hemming was in the habit of saying. "We have no Alps, so it turned out to be weight lifting." And Anette Svensson who had chosen neither weight lifting nor rock climbing felt that she was more and more often occupied with both. She lifted and carried the weight of the Spirit, of Hemming, and of her fault up the hill of Meaninglessness.

If she had ever grown tired she would have greeted weariness as recreation and a letup. The ease with which she carried even the heaviest burden bored her to death.

She was now twenty-eight. And she saw before her the long length of the life that remained, thirty, forty, fifty years of this horrible strength.

How does one free oneself of strength, how does one acquire weakness?

At last she knew, she heard it said within herself: by a repulsive exercise of strength, with a lift so horrible that it could never be repeated, she would be able to secure by force the weakness she needed.

It was a Sunday in May, he wanted to see Stockholm once more from the Katarina lift. She carried him downstairs to the car, drove to Slussen, lifted him over to his wheelchair, took the lift up to the bridge. It was a sunny but cool day with no wind.

She looked at Hemming and the wheelchair and Stockholm.

"Stockholm weighs seventeen billion tons," said Hemming.

"Yes," said Anette Svensson, "there are weights that are completely inhuman."

"All the same everything is held on high," said Hemming.

"Yes," she said. "It is odd."

"As soon as there is anything that needs carrying, a suitable strength is sure to crop up," said Hemming.

"Yes," she said. "There are no doubt enormously many more strengths than we can ever imagine."

"Continents, towns, and people," he said. "Everything is carried. It is no doubt some sort of a law of nature."

She looked at him intently, lately his shoulders had begun to slouch forward, and he smiled all the time.

"At the time I could hold myself up by my own strength I never felt as safe as I do now."

Yes, there sat Hemming and positively shone with trustfulness.

And now Anette Svensson heard something within her pointing out that the time had arrived. She lifted him gently from his wheelchair—he lay warm and thankful against her—she lifted him in outstretched arms above her head, why, he even giggled with titillated delight, and she threw him in a wide arc over the safety railing. She was full of the chill of the Spirit and had no need to exert herself. Later she said to the prosecutor: "Hemming threw himself."

Ahoo.

And while he was falling, while rotating, limp but at the same time struggling, he plunged downward, he cried: "It is not the Holy Spirit! It is not the Holy Spirit!"

But none of the onlookers, the few who happened to be present, took any notice of his cries. They didn't take him seriously. They all saw how clumsy and ugly and deformed his body was, and no one could understand why he was yelling that his was not the Holy Spirit. Everyone knows that the Holy Spirit is a dove who sinks down slowly.

"Have you now said what you want to say about that thing the Spirit?" asks the writer.

"One can never say what one wants to," says the text.

"And Anette Svensson? Why did you lay her open to this devilish illusion?"

"In order to purify her of her innocent lack of a view of life. To bring her to an awareness of it."

"Awareness of it?"

"Yes. I must have some excuse," says the text.

"Of what should she become aware?"

"I don't know. She doesn't even know herself yet, she only sits still in a cell, and a wardress has to feed her, since she cannot think of lifting anything, not even her hands."

"And the Spirit?"

"That," says the text. "Oh, I have put that back in one of the freezer compartments in Åhlen's at Klaraberg Street, the one with fish and shellfish, between the cod and the crab. That was where I got it."

James, the Poor in Spirit

T HIS is how it was: God created the world by speaking
with thirty-two voices. He divided the world into
three books, one for the sea, one for the earth, and one
for the air, and He collected the three books into one volume
which He called the universe. When he spoke with the thirty-
two voices He used twenty-two letters: the three letters that
were the mothers of all the other letters, *alath, mem,* and *shin,*
and in addition seven double letters and twelve single. And
about the world He set a boundary that was the number ten:
Ten that within itself bore the five eternally opposite pairs, the
ten Incompatibles which incessantly strove against each other
and by their strife maintained the eternal movement that is
called life, these ten totally different things that He united into
five indissoluble marriages; east and west, north and south, evil
and goodness, height and depth, beginning and end. And He
Himself lived in the whole that He had created, as fire lives
in coal.

This is the simple way in which existence appeared to
James the son of Alphaeus.

In order to conform with creation in a respectable and
exemplary manner he had himself married Mariam, daughter
of Hurais.

He had paid ten shekels of silver for her, a cheap price. As a bridal gift he had given her ten ells of red linen, a veil, and an enormous spray of myrtle. She hung the spray of myrtle by the door, sewed herself a cloak of the linen, and bore him three sons in the space of three years.

But after that he chanced to become one of the twelve disciples.

Jesus of Nazareth preached that God would soon dissolve His laws, nothing would remain, not the twenty-two letters, nor the sea, the earth and the heavens, not the five pairs of opposites, He would create everything anew. And James wanted to be part of it right from the beginning so that he might with certainty experience the end.

He therefore left Mariam and his three sons in Capernaum, he even left his humble occupation with the town's customs office, he left everything in spite of the fact that Mariam wept and questioned him:

"James, should not our union last forever?"

And James answered: "He shall dissolve everything."

So he joined Peter, Andrew, and the other nine disciples, the Master led and they followed Him.

But Mariam, she who was left behind, first felt peculiar distress; she was filled by a corroding compassion for herself; for two days and two nights she lay unconscious and her three sons sat whimpering beside her bed, but then she got up, she decided to endure, to submit herself to being abandoned.

She carried out into the yard all the little things that had belonged to him and burned them: the tattered sandals, the broken comb he had used for his beard, the spoon of goat's horn, the little red flute, the three-legged post on which his cloak had hung, the flyswatter of plaited grasses, his puttees that he had never used.

When that was done she began to weep again, she wept so much that she went blind for a month; a black animal seemed to be devouring her from within.

And she was struck by dumbness, so that she could not say anything to her three sons, but was obliged to whip and beat them to make them understand her.

The women of Capernaum came to tell her everything that was being said about James; about how he was wandering about the country with the band of disciples, now he was here now he was there, how he was associating with thieves and prostitutes and vagabonds. "Don't grieve for him," they said, "be thankful that you were rid of him at last."

"About whom are you talking?" said Mariam. "James? I had forgotten him."

But the truth was that she longed for him so that she spat blood, and her belly swelled up and became like a faulty wineskin. Her breasts were filled with tiny cracks and a pale milklike liquid oozed from them.

And she had to take down the spray of myrtle once a week from its hook and carry it carefully outside to let the wind blow it free of dust.

After two years had passed these torments were over. James's Master had been executed in Jerusalem, but in spite of this he had not returned home, and she realized that he had not only cast her off, he had forgotten her, and those parts of her body that had previously swelled and overflowed with longing now began to shrink and shrivel with resignation.

As she grew increasingly thin and bony she brought up her three sons. What she needed for the necessities of life she got from her father-in-law Alphaeus, who was deeply ashamed of his wastrel son. She brought up her sons to be timorous, indeed anguished, and in all they did dutiful young men. She succeeded in obtaining places in the Customs Department for two of them; the third became part owner of a fishing boat in Magdala.

In the matter of God's re-creation of the world James became more and more uncertain. Perhaps He had already made everything anew, but in a way that James had not succeeded in discovering. Perhaps it was going to happen in the time to come, in which case it was just a matter of patiently awaiting these coming times. One by one the disciples broke up from Jerusalem—those who had not been killed during the first difficult years. They were to carry His Message to all the four cardinal points, preferably to the four corners of the earth, provided that cardinal points and corners still existed. James was to found a community in Gamala, after that he was to proceed eastward.

He had really completely forgotten Mariam and his three sons.

And he only remembered the Message uncertainly and incompletely.

His preaching was filled with words like *perhaps, it may be, possibly, probably,* and *it may be thought that . . .*

In the end it seemed to him as if just uncertainty and the honest account of irresolution were the Message itself. He never preached about God's thirty-two voices, the three books, the twenty-two letters, the ten pairs of opposites, no, not even once about the Law; perhaps all had been got rid of and destroyed, perhaps not.

He was poor in spirit, that was all he knew. That knowledge made him exceedingly humble. And that humility made him devout, yes, he was the most devout man in Gamala.

Unfortunately his preaching did not win him any devoted followers. But he got a number of friends. His friends became his congregation, they congregated around his devoutness.

And he never got farther than to Gamala. There in confidence and doubt he awaited the final remolding of existence.

His back became bent, his hair and beard turned white, he stopped eating, he had no need of other nourishment than humility and devoutness. He ceased to speak, he delivered the Message with his eyes and with the careful movement of his hands, he had forgotten the name of the devil and he finally died a virgin.

On the morning that Mariam got to hear that he was dead and was lying in state in Gamala she took down the spray of myrtle from its place by the door—it was now stained with mildew— she dressed herself in the red linen cloak, on her feet she bound her toughest sandals, and then she set off. She walked with great strength and determination, bending forward with long strides, her knees bent. She swung the spray of myrtle in her right hand, now and then she used it as a stick to help her to walk faster—she was afraid they would have time to bury him—her red cloak flapped in the wind from the Lake of Gennesar.

By evening she had arrived. She stood by his bier.

His hands were clasped over his breast, his aged head gleamed with peace; she could clearly see that he had undoubtedly forgotten her long ago.

She gazed at him; his friends, those he was in the habit of calling his congregation, drew back timorously when they felt the fearful chill that emanated from her, they retreated and left her alone with him, wife with husband.

Her face, that face which had once been gentle and bright, so gentle and so bright that, before he became an apostle, James had not been able to withstand it, that face was now dark and harsh. Mortification and bitterness, which had been her only distraction for many years, had scratched it and lined it and covered it with dark streaks.

When they had been left alone she moved up to the head of the bier, she bent over him and recited three times with a strange tenderness in her voice a curse over the man who, because of falseness and faithlessness, will never be granted one day of rest or satisfaction or refreshment in the realm of death. Then she spat in his face seven times, seven good mouthfuls of sticky saliva and expectoration. Finally she lifted up the spray of myrtle, that withered bone-dry spray of myrtle, and rammed it with all the strength she had into his right eye, rammed it so hard it was not halted until it reached the bone at the back of his neck.

And James felt that the final upheaval had at last taken place. To him it seemed that everything was suddenly made anew, that unimaginable wealth and heavenly joy had come to him, understanding that would endure for eternity. He felt as if he were a coal in whose innermost being fire dwelt.

To have had something to abandon, something that even in your very bones you can blot out by abandoning! To have owned someone whose love showed itself to be as inextinguishable as the deepest hatred! To have been the object of a love which even in death refused to let itself be rejected.

And he sat up, he rose from the deathbed on which he lay. He dried the horrid curse and the sticky spittle from his face, the dry mildewy spray of myrtle still stuck out of his eye, he stood up and faced her, took her in his arms, and made love to her on the spot.

The Way
of a Serpent

Translated by
Tom Geddes

Appendix to the Secretary's Annual Report to the Västerbotten County Agricultural Society, 1882.

In the course of my journey along the valley of the Vindel River in October last I devoted one day to visiting the place close to the boundary between the parishes of Lycksele and Norsjö known as Slough Hill, where a minor natural disaster is said to have occurred in the middle of the last decade. A young woman, Tilda Markström, who runs the local village shop, guided me to the spot. She maintained that her father, Karl Markström, a shopkeeper, had perished there in a landslide. To what extent this accords with the truth is, however, a matter on which I will not speculate. The inhabitants of these godforsaken backwoods have an unfortunate tendency to prefer stories to actual reality; these people lack all understanding of scientific principles.

That a landslide has occurred here would nevertheless seem to be indisputable. The escarpment of the landslide has a length of some 300 ells, the collapsed mass of soil, predominantly composed of boulders and moraine gravel, seems to have largely disappeared into the marsh that lies below the escarpment. No trace of habitations or the like is to be observed, but the higher ground would appear to have been cultivated from time to time.

The local populace do not seem to have made any significant observations; they do not recall any fissuring, subsidence, or the like which might be consistent with the event, they appear simply to believe that God's creation and transformation of the world goes on continuously. Creation is (according to them) an unending process.

The place has acquired the name New Hollow. The word hollow in this part of the country signifies a depression or valley of not very considerable extent. Its location is marked on the attached map with the symbol ╁.

Umeå, 11th December, 1882.
Rutger Bygdelius.
Secretary to the Västerbotten County Agricultural Society.

O Lord, was it him, Karl Orsa the farmer and shop-keeper, you wanted to bury that time when you tore apart Slough Hill like that, or was it me and my house and Johanna? And the children who had not yet lived their lives?

It doesn't happen in these parts, they say. Earthquakes, chasms, upheavals. Never.

That is all I want to ask.

You know my circumstances.

The language I am speaking to you in, O Lord, I learned at Baggböle, from Jacob.

Circumstances is a grand word.

I will tell you the whole story, Lord, I will tell you the whole story from beginning to end, and then I will ask you about the things that I do not understand.

Johan Johansson is my name, called Bragging Johnny by the folks around here—and probably known by that name even to you, who make no distinctions between people—born at Slough Hill in 1849, the year that my mother's father, Alexis, hanged himself in one of Ol Karlsa's pine trees—he had no forest of his own left by then—and the same year that two of Johan Olof's bulls drowned in the spring near Farm Marsh and so gave it its name, the Ox Spring—because everything has to have a name.

If you, Lord, ever need a scoop of water that will quench the thirst of an eternal being, then I advise you to go to the Ox Spring. It's as clear and cold as the air between the stars and it's just ten paces from the last footbridge before Fir Hill.

You know that I was born defiant, you created me defiant. And you've always spoken to me and said: Do not be defiant, Bragging Johnny. You are strange like that, you form us in a very particular way, boastful or pigheaded or whatever, and then you use up our lives telling us that is exactly what we should not be, we're not to be the particular way you created us.

But on the other hand, you were fair in not giving me very much to vent my defiance on. If you'd made me the son of a shopkeeper or a big farmer then I might have become a dangerous man, with all that stubbornness and obstinacy built into me, I could have been a difficult master; but in the circumstances you put me in my defiance was so slight and ineffectual that it seemed no more than a wasting disease within me. Lord, to whom shall we go?

It's almost like an abyss you made here at Slough Hill, and as I'm sitting now my legs hang down over the chasm, I don't feel any fear, after what happened I can hang my legs over any precipice, I know that you can open up abysses wherever and whenever you fancy, and even here above the abyss—or whatever this great hole ought to be called—I can feel defiance within me. He restoreth my soul, He leadeth me in the paths of righteousness for His name's sake.

No, you let me be born without any father at all, and that was probably just as well, we'd have had to find food for him too—you gave me indifference at birth to water down the defiance with—and he can't have been much of a man, because you took him to the asylum at Pitholmen and there he just faded away and died.

But in his stead we did have this harmonium that Rönn, Mother's godfather, the carpenter from Tjöln, had built for her and that sometimes earned us a crust of bread with its flighty tunes, especially if you pulled out the stops called Principal and Flute.

And one of them shall not fall on the ground without your Father. But the very hairs of your head are all numbered.

They used to fetch Mother on Saturday evenings when she'd done the milking, they'd be raucous and merry, they would carry out the harmonium and put it on a flat wagon or a sleigh, and put Mother, who was part and parcel of their fun, next to the driver, and then they'd drive off to some outhouse or kitchen or barn and there they would dance right through to morning milking, and we used to be woken up when they lifted the harmonium down at the front door steps and when Mother clattered the rings on the stove.

He didn't have any forest of his own, my grandfather, nor any upland plots or meadow, not a scrap did he have, although he wasn't born without any. But he wasted the whole lot, the sedge meadow and the ploughland, Meadow Hill and the Rocklands. And when he'd lost everything he fell into poverty and want.

Yet he was as innocent as a newborn babe, he didn't drink spirits, he just frittered away his property like a little child walking about on the grass scattering behind him whatever he had in his hands. He was easygoing and good-natured and careless, he made his deals with Ol Karlsa—you have to do business, he would say—there were horseshoes and horseshoe

nails and axes and saw blades and salt and sugar and iron for
the smithy and weaving reeds for Grandmother.

He had no money, but things could always be pawned or
mortgaged. Ol Karlsa had printed bonds all ready. The
ploughland and Meadow Hill and the sedge meadow and the
Rocklands, and another day, and tomorrow—yes, precisely:
another day and a tomorrow would come when he would have
to repay these small sums with interest. But the year before I
was born, Lord, you let Ol Karlsa come along with the bonds,
carrying them in Bible covers from which he'd removed the
Word of God and put in all his own papers tied with leather
straps. It was a Sunday, and Grandfather said that it made him
glad to see a shopkeeper who observed the day of rest with
such grace and devotion that he carried the Word with him
under his arm wherever he went.

"You're a mighty pious shopkeeper," he said.

Shopkeeper is what Grandfather said, though Ol Karlsa
was really an ordinary farmer like himself, it was only through
loansharking that he'd started dealing in all kinds of goods and
had become a kind of trader. And why, Lord, did you set
farmers to rule this glorious earth that you created and why
did you fill them with wickedness and low cunning and lust
for power so they aren't like human beings at all?

"It's the bonds," said Ol Karlsa. "I've had the Word of
the Lord re-bound in ox hide."

"Ah," said Grandfather, "it's the bonds you're out walking with."

And he went on innocently:

"Mother could give us a drop of beer if we go inside, it's
a week old and just at its best."

But Ol Karlsa put on a show of reluctance, he'd drunk
at the spring by Fir Hill and on Sundays he wouldn't touch
beer if it was fermented, and it was cash he was after right now,
and it was marvelous how well the barley was coming on here

on the hillside, but it must be the sun and the lack of wind.

"But we can sit ourselves down anyway," said Grandfather.

When he was sitting Ol Karlsa said:

"Aye. These bonds."

"I haven't any cash," said Grandfather. "I'll have some by and by."

"I'm going into Skellefteå tomorrow," said Ol Karlsa. "I'll be taking the bonds with me."

"I think you're right about the barley," said Grandfather. "Always in the lee and plenty of sun."

But by and by, he said, by and by he would clear the land behind the barn, another patch of barley, and he would dig a ditch right down the hillside and a bit into the marsh and there he could have a hayfield and some grazing, he'd warrant that by and by crops and cash, and calves and kids and lambs and skins and God's mercy and blessing . . .

But Ol Karlsa wouldn't accept by and by, he even had an almanac with him and that just had names of days and months but not by and by. Debt recovery proceedings and courts and registration of title had their months and days and to every thing there is a season, and a time to every purpose under the heaven. A time to plant and a time to pluck up that which is planted. A time to kill, and a time to heal, a time to break down, and a time to build up. A time to weep, a time to laugh. And a time to mourn. But for by and by? There's none for by and by.

"Why didn't you kill him?" Grandmother said afterward.

"It didn't occur to me," said Grandfather.

She thought of the strength he had in him and you know it too: he had performed miracles, carried a hundredweight sack on his outstretched arms, stood under the belly of a mare and heaved her up, lifted two fully grown men on the palms of his hands, straightened out a number nine horseshoe—

though no one knows if there were any such shire horses here
in those days.

"But why didn't you kill him?" said Grandmother.

"That just wasn't the way it went," said Grandfather.

In the autumn, in October, after the threshing, in the
middle of the shearing and before the days of baking the bread,
Ol Karlsa arrived with the title deed.

"Crofter or freeholder," he said, "you'll always be the
same, Alexis. And now I've got what is mine. And you've paid
your way. Like a man. And I can buy the wool. And if you
do have any beer . . . And we can come to terms about the
rent. And if I buy the wool it will be for cash. Cash for the
rent."

"Rent?" said Grandfather. "For my own place?"

"For my place," said Ol Karlsa and brought out the title
deed. "We can come to terms, I'm sure. We've always come
to terms.

"I'm not a wicked man," he added—but Grandfather
could see wickedness glinting in his eyes.

Why didn't he kill him, that's what I say to you, Lord,
and you probably say the same thing: Why didn't he kill him!
Ol Karlsa was sixty-one, Grandfather getting on for fifty-
seven, and Ol Karlsa's soul was bound in the bundle of life
with the Lord, but Grandfather's wasn't.

My mother, she was seventeen that autumn, she brought
out the beer and they came to terms about the rent and
Grandfather said that the other children, Lina and Eva and
Tilda and Maria and Alida, they had gone out into the world
now and it was only she, Thea, who was left and she had this
gift for music and the harmonium that Rönn from Tjöln had
built for her, and she played a hymn.

"There'll always be a way to manage," said Ol Karlsa.
"But you should have had a boy."

"That just wasn't the way it went," said Grandfather. "She plays, and the others dance."

□

Let's start from the beginning.

About paying rent. Back in '49, the first autumn of my life, Grandfather went over to Skellefteå with the mirror, his own wedding ring and Grandmother's, and the porcelain cock Grandmother had got as wages in service at Böle, and it was just enough.

But by the next year he couldn't see how to cope.

Dear Lord: paying rent!

One year, the year of mourning, was rent-free for those of us who were left, Mother and Grandmother and myself, and I had just learned to walk.

"I'm not an evil man," said Ol Karlsa. "This year I'll let you have it gratis and for nothing. As ye have freely received, so shall ye also freely give."

But the next autumn Mother had to find it all herself. She was twenty then.

"Where would we get the money from?" Mother asked.

But Ol Karlsa just leered at her, you know how he used to leer. He took out his watch and leered at her as if the time had something to do with the rent. It was the middle of the day, and he leered at Grandmother and me and then at Mother again.

"What's his name?" he said.

"Johan," said mother. "After his dad's father."

"So he has a grandfather on his father's side," said Ol Karlsa.

"Of course he has," said Grandmother. "A grandfather. Of course he has."

He grew fat in his last few years, did Ol Karlsa. He

wanted to possess everything, even that: rolls of fat on his neck, bags of lard under his eyes, lumps of tallow on his fingers, blobs of fat everywhere—he should lack nothing.

"Money," he said. "I have that already. Enough and to spare."

That was a strange thing to say. It was the first time in his life that he'd said it. He was getting at something.

Unto everyone that hath shall be given, and he shall have abundance; but from him that hath not shall be taken away even that which he hath. It was quite clear what he was thinking.

"And firewood," he went on. "You two poor women and no man. No, there can't be any question of money."

If there was ever a time when you, Lord, should have intervened, it was then, that was the right moment for your providence, but nothing happened, nothing in particular. Grandmother prayed silently so hard that her whole face wrinkled up, and Mother grabbed her hymnbook and held it to her belly as if to protect herself. But Ol Karlsa sat down on the woodbin and said:

"Won't you play for me, Thea?"

And that wasn't much to ask; music is a sort of comfort, and while you're playing it's as if you're given a respite from other things. She played hymns and pieces from "Songs of the Lamb" and he seemed to enjoy listening to them. He shut his eyes and waggled his shoes up and down—the farmers here have always been partial to music—and for a while Grandmother thought he would be content with this and fall asleep.

But in the middle of "Out of the depths have I cried, O Lord. Lord, hear my voice: let thine ears be attentive to the voice of my supplications," he roused himself, got up, stepped across to Mother, and pushed in all the stops so that the harmonium suddenly fell silent, and he told Grandmother to take the little boy, poor thing, and go outside, for now he was going to settle this matter of the rent and it would be quite enough if he just had Thea to settle the business with.

And you, Lord, who had also created Ol Karlsa, you know how he collected that rent, you weren't caught unawares by it. The foldaway bed was at the far end of the kitchen, and that's where he claimed his rights and we won't argue about those rights. He was as slow and long-winded and clumsy as an old boar and, Lord, to whom shall we go?

At that time, on his first such visit, I was two, Mother was twenty, Karl Orsa, his son, was twenty-eight, and Grandmother had only two years left.

Later in the autumn he came with two loads of birchwood and half a sack of salt and a pair of shoes from Skellefteå for Mother. Thou shalt by no means come out thence till thou hast paid the uttermost farthing, and Mother paid our way, for we've never had any choice but to pay our way.

Karl Orsa, the son, he was different. He never said a word and he was tall and thin and kind of gloomy; he never joined in when they fetched the harmonium and Mother, he never learned to dance, and why should he have danced, he had enough as it was, two and a half thousand acres of forest, fifty acres of ploughland, Hill Marsh and Long Marsh for hay, thirteen cows in the barn and two horses and the shop and he was going to have it all to himself, so he had no need to dance.

You can't see the bottom from up here on the edge, Lord, that's how deep this pit is that you made. It's called New Hollow, it was called New Hollow in the first year, everything has to have a name, and nobody knew afterward who was the first to call it that.

When Mother realized that she was in the family way, you, Lord, put it into her mind to go to Ol Karlsa. He had running sores on one leg now and sat in the parlor behind the shop. It was the beginning of spring and there was muddy water pouring from Mother's boots. She'd also had in mind to say that they, she and Ol Karlsa, had brought it on themselves to be expecting a little 'un together. She had a craving and was eating salt straight from the sack.

"Can't be true," he said, rubbing his leg. "I'm old and my hands are shaking. And now I've got leg sores."

And he mentioned his wife too:

"Haven't even been near Magda these last two years," he said.

"Our Lord knows how this happened," said Mother. "What you've got us into. It's because of the rent that you took."

"The rent?" he said.

"Yes, the rent," Mother said.

"It's easy enough to see you're in the family way," he said. "And even if there's no father for the young 'un he does at least have a grandfather. Of course he has."

And Mother had to defend herself:

"Johan does have a father. It's down in the parish register. But he fell ill. He was taken away to Pitholmen. The asylum."

"I'm in the process of handing things over," said Ol Karlsa. "I hand over a little bit each day. The forest. And the ploughland. And the shop. And the hay meadows."

"And you're handing over me and mine as well?"

"I'm handing over everything. When you have running sores you didn't ought to hold on to anything. Once you get leg sores you should step aside."

"And you're sure it's leg sores?" said Mother.

"If it isn't something even worse," said Ol Karlsa. "But if it's the will of the Lord."

You know he always spoke like that.

"You'll have to come to an arrangement with my boy, Karl Orsa. About the rent. I'm done with all that now," he said. "But he won't be unreasonable, I'm sure. Though of course . . . if it weren't for the leg sores . . . And you can take a sugarloaf for your boy. Or two. Take two sugarloaves."

His last few months were hard for Ol Karlsa, it was a kind of justice, the running sores spread up his legs and over his belly and chest and arms and head and he couldn't take his food anymore. And he knew that the only thing to keep meat fresh is salt, so he got Magda to cover his sores with coarse salt every day, morning and evening. It was dreadfully painful at first and he screamed terribly, but gradually his flesh got used to the salt, and in his last few days the pain seemed to have stopped, but by then he was so far gone that it was no longer any comfort. Karl Orsa put the funeral off till Michaelmas, since the corpse was already salted anyway, he said, and it was a thundery summer when all the work seemed to take three times as long as usual.

My sister, my first sister, was born in the middle of summer, and she was called Eva after one of my mother's sisters. Mother seemed really glad to have her—you, Lord, understand these things better than I do—and she used to carry her to the meadows in the birchbark sling on her back that Grandfather had made while she was expecting me. She was light in color like us, not dark like Ol Karlsa's family. "And I'll teach her to play," said Mother, "I'll teach her to play light music."

□

"This was for you," said Karl Orsa when he came that autumn after taking over everything that Ol Karlsa had left him.

"It was probably made in Italy," he said. "Or Palestine. My old man started talking about it the last day his head was clear. 'I want Thea to have the mirror,' he said. 'As a sort of memento. I've always liked her music. The mirror with the snails and crystals and shellfish on the frame. The one I bought in Piteå when I sold the dog skins to the Crown.' "

And Mother just took the mirror and hung it on the nail that had been left there ever since her father had left with the old mirror.

"Leave the nail there," Grandfather had said. "You never know."

Just as if he had sensed it: there will be another mirror one day.

"That's a fine-looking mirror, that is," said Grandmother.

"What's her name?" said Karl Orsa, nodding in the direction of the baby girl.

"Eva," said Mother. "After her aunt who went down to Umeå to go into service with a clergyman. She's in a place called Ön."

Did he realize that it was his own sister he was looking at? Mother could have said it, she should have said it, but she looked at the mirror and that just wasn't the way it went.

Lord, putting things into proper words is hard, how do you say at a loss?

"But the rent," Mother said. "Did he remember to say anything about the rent at the end?"

"Only the mirror," said Karl Orsa. "He had already handed over the shop and the farm. Before he died it was mainly just little things that he still had to sort out. All that remained were unimportant little things and death."

He was thirty and a mature man, was Karl Orsa. He had dark brown hair with a slightly fairer fringe of beard that was always neatly trimmed, he stood stiff and straight, and he wore a frock coat and moved slowly, he would never do anything hastily or needlessly.

"I'll sit down and check the book after New Year," he said. "And we'll see about the rent then."

"So there was a book, then?" Mother said.

"It's all written down," said Karl Orsa. "He was very particular, the old man. And for this year it's been paid up. He's written that down in the book."

"I was thinking more about by and by," said Mother. "I'm on my own. And no money."

"If it weren't for the shop," said Karl Orsa. "But the shop can't be run without cash. Otherwise there'd be no need for money. But I have to have it for the shop."

And before leaving he added:

"But you can always have credit. If you need it. It'll be all right."

On Boxing Day they came to fetch Mother and the harmonium, to go dancing at Ristjöln, and she took Eva with her in the sling, she needed to be breast-fed.

She brought a fellow back home with her from Ristjöln. He came on skis behind the sleigh where Mother and Eva sat in sheepskin rugs and behind the sledge carrying the harmonium. His name was Jacob and he had only one eye. And he was a southerner: he said himself that he came from the land of Canaan but it was probably no further than Ångermanland or at most Småland.

Lord, it was you that had sent him.

"He didn't dance," said Mother. "He looked after the baby for me over at Ristjöln. Not a single dance."

He'd come to Umeå on a boat. He'd worked for a timber merchant there. He'd been a farmhand at Sävar. And barked poles for hayracks at Röbäck. And last autumn he'd been squaring timber at Burträsk. And now he'd come north with a carter. Grandmother asked about the eye but he didn't really explain it, he just held his hand over the empty eye socket and said he'd lost it but could see quite well with the one he still had, he didn't expect too much. He was a small, thin man with sloping shoulders, he had a quick and easy laugh, especially when he played with Eva, and on the very first day he arrived he carved me a toy man that could stand and rock on the edge of the table. He had hardly anything in his rucksack, just a plane and a rasp and knives and two chisels; no, he was nothing special, was Jacob, rather the opposite. He was just the man mother needed.

When Karl Orsa came over at Epiphany Jacob brought out a leather pouch straightaway and paid the rent. For which of you, intending to build a tower, sitteth not down first, and counteth the cost, whether he have sufficient to finish it? Rejoice with me; for I have found the piece which I had lost!

"So some money has come into the house," said Karl Orsa. "Real big money."

And Mother seemed neither to see nor hear, she went over to the harmonium and began to play, and Karl Orsa stood for a while as if he was embarrassed and confused. He should have said something more but that just wasn't the way it went. He put the money in his coat pocket and leered at Mother, and she trod the pedals faster than usual and played "I neither gold nor wealth possess, My lot in life is humble, But I my heavenly Father bless, Though I on earth may stumble," and Grandmother went up to this Jacob whom she hardly knew and stroked his cheek as if he was a little child, and it seemed as if the business of the rent was now finished with for good and all.

Seven years he stayed, did Jacob. He even bought a cow. He had wages outstanding at Burträsk and he went there and fetched a cow and paid a bit extra to make up the difference. It was a black cow and she was called Angel. He could do most things, he mended the shoes and made rakes and coffins for people and he squared timber for folks who were going to build, he made two lots of wood tar, and made the barrels himself, and he fished and nailed up pike to dry on the wall of the barn. But he couldn't hunt or shoot: it was his aiming eye that he'd lost. And mother had two girls by him, Rachel and Sarah. And he got himself two Lapland dog bitches to breed, and they had eight pups altogether, and he kept them in an enclosure all winter so they turned wild, and in the spring he slaughtered them and prepared the skins and when autumn came he made a fur coat for Mother, so that she wouldn't freeze to death when she traveled around with the harmonium, and dog-skin gloves for her playing hands.

And he always made sure there was money to pay the rent with, he was careful about that, although it wasn't in his nature to be careful about anything, and he had a weakness for gin. He got it from Karl Orsa who brought it in casks from Skellefteå. Jacob would buy a jar at a time and then drink it until it was finished, which would take about three days, and afterward he was like a little child, crying and sorrowful and wanting us to forgive him, although he hadn't done anything evil, and Mother had to play some "Songs of the Lamb" for him so that it sounded like a prayer meeting, and it was strange that such a small man could drink so heartily and call so loudly and powerfully to God.

Do you remember that I used to call him Father?

"You can call Jacob Father," said Mother, "he deserves something for all his hard work, and we must try to give him some of the little we have so that he won't feel dissatisfied. We should always do what we can," she added.

So I called him Father, though I only ever thought of him as Jacob.

Karl Orsa drank gin too. But not like Jacob so that he got drunk and sentimental and childish, just a small dram each day to stop his rigid body from seizing up completely and to help him cope with speaking to people. He was so serious and somber in his thoughts that it was hard for him to talk, and he never laughed except when he had to.

In the autumn of the first year that Jacob was with us Grandmother fell ill, it was in her belly and caused her terrible pain, you, Lord, know what it was but we supposed it was cancer, and she couldn't take food and had to stay in bed for two months and just before Christmas she died. And it was mostly Jacob who looked after her, he seemed to be used to it in the same way that he seemed to be used to almost everything, it was he who lifted her up and bathed her back when it got sore and it was he who managed to keep her just alive with gruel and combed her hair and read her the Psalms and the Epistles to the Corinthians and when she was dead he washed her once more and it was he who made the coffin for her. We then that are strong ought to bear the infirmities of the weak, and not to please ourselves.

In the autumn of 1860, when I was eleven, Mother was twenty-nine, Eva eight, Sarah five, and Rachel three, they came to fetch Jacob. What the reason was they didn't say but it was something that had happened on the boat he'd come to Umeå on. It was thanks to Karl Orsa that they found him—he'd gone to a lot of trouble in Skellefteå, had Karl Orsa, to find out who Jacob really was, and it turned out that they'd been looking for him all these years. The last thing he did at our place was to give Mother the money for the next year's rent.

They took Jacob in the sleigh; the skis that he'd come on were left behind and so was Angel, the cow. The same evening Karl Orsa came and said that the fact was that Jacob was a thief, that he'd stolen money on that boat and before that he'd stolen a lot of things, thieving was part of his nature.

"But you're in credit," he told Mother. "You haven't got a man now but I'll give you credit."

And Mother, she paid the rent in advance for the next year and said that she hadn't known that he was a thief, he hadn't stolen anything at our place, no, he'd given more than he'd taken, although there wasn't much to take of course, and that the only thing that mattered to her was just to do what she could.

"Can't you play a tune for me, Thea?" said Karl Orsa.

"No," said Mother. "I'm still free of debt. But the day I owe you something, then I'll play for you. Then you'll have a right to the music. But not until then."

□

In '62, just after New Year, Karl Orsa arrived. He came empty-handed except that he brought a sugarloaf for Sarah and Rachel, he was in no hurry to broach his business, he wore his frock coat as if he was out for a Sunday walk.

I was thirteen, although I wasn't big, I'd been ditching over at Home Farm Marsh all autumn and got food and a half farmhand's wages and Mother had been playing every weekend, she was turned thirty now and the harmonium had lost a stop and Rönn was dead so it wasn't repaired.

"We'll manage all right now," she said when I came home with the money.

That was typical of her: We'll manage all right now.

"Though we haven't paid the rent," she added. "If only the rent wasn't still due."

"He's been out to work," said Karl Orsa. "Your boy Johnny. Well now."

And Mother brought out the money and laid it on the corner of the table and told him to count it, she hadn't been able to count this big pile herself. He could take what was owing for the rent, what was left over she'd use for all the other expenses and food and clothes and salt for the food and the bone buttons and salt herring that she'd taken on tick from his shop.

But he barely looked at the money, he leered at Mother and unbuttoned his coat and buttoned it up again and smoothed down his hair and fidgeted with his feet as if he was cold or needed to pee.

"Is that all your money?" he said. "That lot?"

"Don't you have the heart to take it, Karl Orsa?" Mother said. "You needn't feel sorry for us. Right's right."

"I don't have to count it," he said. "I can see from here that it's not half the rent. And I won't take your last pennies. You keep 'em. I'm not an evil man."

"By and by," I said. "By and by I'll be going ditching again. And I'll dig another patch behind the barn. By and by. And maybe manage to afford a horse. And I might even get a tar still. By and by."

But they didn't hear me, I was too small and weedy, my voice was too feeble, they didn't even look at me, Mother didn't dare to.

Therefore I take pleasure in infirmities, in reproaches, in necessities, in persecutions, in distresses: for when I am weak, then am I strong.

"Angel," Mother said. "Our cow. You can take her."

But Karl Orsa didn't say anything, it wasn't Angel he was after, nor the cash; but every man is tempted when he is drawn away of his own lust and enticed, it was Mother he was after.

"A whole cow," said Mother. "If that isn't enough I don't know what is."

But he made a show of reluctance, it was as if he had to be coaxed into accepting that cow.

"The hay will be gone by March anyway," said Mother. "We're a bit short. And what are we to do then? You may as well take her. She'll only be a burden to us by spring."

And in the end he had to turn his attention to this damned cow.

"I suppose I'll have to go and take a look at her then," he said. "That's not to say . . . But since you insist, Thea."

And in the barn he pinched Angel hard, inspected her legs, and ran his hand over her back.

"How old would she be?" he asked.

"She'll be ten this autumn," said Mother.

"She's a bit thin and scraggy," said Karl Orsa.

And that was the truth, there was nothing special about our cow, Angel. An old cow, a bit down in the mouth and listless.

Lord, you knew Angel too. That's how it was.

And Karl Orsa examined her udder.

"Little sores on the teats," he said. "And the udder is empty."

Then he leered at Mother, her bosom was full and firm. You could see he was thinking, Those tits.

"What about for slaughter?" Mother tried. "For butchering?"

Then he had to go over Angel with his hands and eyes again, he knew a thing or two about butcher's meat as well.

"She hasn't much meat on her," he said. "She's not much more than skin and bone. Like an empty hayrick. Scrawny little beast."

And he made eyes at Mother again and you could see he was thinking, Flesh.

Mother's final suggestion was:

"The skin? A cowhide at least?"

But it didn't even seem worth considering:

"Hides don't sell. Nobody's buying hides. Especially cowhides. There's more hide than live animals. No point at all."

He made eyes at Mother's skin too, she had bare arms and a bare neck and you could see he'd made his mind up how the rent was to be paid this year.

He would have the music, of course. Eva was ten now, she was the one who had to play, perhaps Mother had spoken to her, and she played dance music and hymns and a tune that Mother had made up herself, and it sounded sort of simpler and merrier from her than when Mother played, and when she had finished playing the new tune, Karl Orsa said:

"I haven't heard that piece before. It was kind of sad even though it went fast."

"I made up that piece myself," Mother said. "It's called 'Karl Orsa's Polka.' "

Everything has to have a name, somebody says the name and that's how it stays, for whatsoever Adam called every living creature, that was the name thereof. "Karl Orsa's Polka."

And afterward, when Eva had played till he'd had his fill of music, I took Eva and Sarah and Rachel with me out to the barn and we sat up close to Angel who at any rate was marvelously warm, and Eva said a poem that she had learned by heart, she was extraordinary when it came to learning things by heart: "Thou, whose heart divine did bleed For the sake of souls untold, Thou who succors those in need And whose arms the babes enfold! Jesu! from all worldly cares By thy guidance I am freed, And my eyes with blissful tears Greet in thee a friend indeed. Why then do I yet despair And from secret torments smart? Danger, Lord! surrounds me here, Frail and helpless is my heart. Do not leave me, for this world Would me from thy love withdraw, From its vain foundations hurled Keep my faith forevermore. Make of woman's heart the shrine Where thy love most brightly burns, Let her feelings gently shine Where a mind uneasy turns. May her hands to those in pain Cups of solace kindly reach, In a world of strife and strain May she comfort bring to each."

Lord, to whom shall we go?

About Angel, while I remember it: she lived to sixteen. Then she got colic and had to be slaughtered and was buried hide and all, as we didn't know for sure.

I stood at the door of the barn and kept watch and saw

him leave. It didn't show on him that he'd collected the rent, he didn't seem to be carrying anything, just the opposite: he was swinging his legs in an unusual way and waving his arms about almost as if it was he who'd paid out something and freed himself from debt.

And when we came in again Mother was sitting at the harmonium. "Be not dismayed if brutal force High honor is accorded, And those who show the least remorse So often are rewarded. For Death shall one day reap them all And they like grass to earth will fall, And wither and be trampled."

And I found the glue pot that Jacob had put away under the floor of the barn, and glued back that stop on the harmonium, Melodia.

□

Zuleima, who she was I don't know. Nobody knows anything, and I really have enquired, but no one, not even the parson. She has a cloth around her hair and something like a shawl over her shoulders and she's holding a tall narrow water jug in front of her and her dress is white. She was on the first page of the almanac in '63.

Lord, do you know who Zuleima is?

Karl Orsa started with the almanacs in '63. He bought them in Skellefteå. On the second page after Zuleima it said that they cost fourteen öre and that it was Norstedts and Sons who had made them, he gave them to his biggest customers and his name was stamped on the cover and he gave them to Mother as a kind of receipt.

If they'd put a headcloth around Mother's hair and dressed her in a white dress and a motley shawl and if they'd put her in the almanac she would have looked like Zuleima. What a handsome woman she was!

There is a Zuleima at Risliden, I've often heard people

mention her, but she was born in '63 and must have been christened after the almanac.

For the first week, right across the whole week from New Year's Day to Epiphany, through Abel and Enoch and Titus and Simeon, he had carefully written DEBT PAID and then he had signed his own name on Augustus's day, when the moon was in the first quarter.

Mother wouldn't accept the almanac at first.

"What do I need it for?" she said. "I never read the almanac. And you're surely not giving it away for nothing? You must have something in mind, Karl Orsa."

"Not at all," he said. "But the children can have it to leaf through. And to look at the letters."

"I don't want to be guilty of more debt than I already am," said Mother and tried to slip the almanac into his hand.

But he backed off toward the door and drew his hand away and said that it might well be that whosoever shall keep the whole law and yet offend in one point, he is guilty of all, and that no one was totally free of debt.

"So take the almanac and keep it, Thea," he said.

We must have had some fifteen almanacs altogether over the years, and we got used to the almanacs just the same as we got used to everything else, if we hadn't received them we'd probably have missed them—the last almanac is in my pocket, 1877—and in all of them was written DEBT PAID.

Jacob had taught me my letters and how to talk properly.

He wrote them with bits of charcoal on the wall of the barn, the second time he was with us he pulled the wall down and moved it a few feet and then the logs were turned around and his letters were separated and disappeared. Although by then I didn't need them anymore. That we should serve in newness of spirit, and not in the oldness of the letter.

So that's how things were; but the almanac still gave us pleasure.

"King Charles XV ascended the throne on 8th July 1859."
"Of the four eclipses, namely two of the sun and two of the
moon, which are due to occur this year, only the second eclipse
of the moon will be visible in these regions." "The market at
Lycksele will be held on 10th January" and "Unless letters
between all inland post offices be franked with postage stamps
to the value of twelve öre at single letter rate they cannot be
accepted for dispatch."

Otherwise, they were years of scarcity then, interminable
winters and frost in August and snow at midsummer and ice
on Longwater on the 17th of June, St. Botolph's Day. To
whom shall we go?

"The fertility of arable land depends on its composition
and suitability for the plants cultivated thereon," you, Lord,
wrote in the almanac. "Only when all the conditions are
fulfilled for the abundant reproduction of the plants cultivated
may rich and profitable harvests be obtained from our arable
fields."

Mother stripped off sallow leaves and we picked horsetail
and sedge from the mere on Rough Marsh and she poured
boiling water on it and made bran for Angel, and we had credit
with Karl Orsa as well. And whenever things were at their
worst, for us in our way and for Karl Orsa in his way, he
would come to find Mother and when he left our debts were
wiped out. Owe no man any thing, but to love one another:
for he that loveth another hath fulfilled the law.

"From small and insignificant seeds all living things
evolve and increase and ultimately multiply and surpass the
mother seed," as you wrote so beautifully in the almanac, Lord.
"That is the very miracle of life itself, the miracle of fertiliza-
tion and growth and birth, which enables human beings to
draw their sustenance from the soil. From a turnip seed no
larger than a small grain of sand we obtain, within a few

months of sowing it, a turnip weighing several pounds, not including its profuse and luxuriant haulms."

In April of '64, on Elias's day, Mother bore Karl Orsa a daughter, she was given the name Tilda, in the parish register Karl Orsa was given the name Father Unknown. That spring I worked on paring down tar stumps for Nicanor in Böle, he was going to make three tar stills that summer. I got food and a laborer's wages but I still didn't earn enough for the rent. I was fifteen. So that's how things were.

When Tilda was born Karl Orsa brought a china plate for her. The edge of the plate was marked in gold letters LOUISA JOSEPHINA EUGENIA.

"She's going to be called Tilda," Mother said. "Not Louisa or anything else."

"It's a royal person," said Karl Orsa. "Louisa Josephina Eugenia. A princess of some kind."

He'd grown side-whiskers now and wasn't completely upright any longer but had begun to stoop a little as if he was always watching his step in a particular way, you could almost see that he was a shopkeeper and that he was constantly working something out, for he who observeth the wind shall not sow; and he that regardeth the clouds shall not reap.

"What's the idea of this plate?" asked Mother. "Is it meant to be some kind of receipt?"

But that seemed to startle him and he dodged the question.

"I just thought you might like it," he said. "It's made in Germany. Genuine bone china."

"So it's not because you're her father?"

"Who the father of your children is the Lord alone knows," he said, and he almost sounded dejected as if he thought that really was the case.

"But you're the only one who's come along with a china plate," Mother remarked.

"It's only by way of a memento," said Karl Orsa. "I do own your place, Thea, and we are acquainted, after all."

And Mother didn't want to argue anymore, that's how things were, and she let it all run off her and she brought out the smoked meat and beer and said to Eva:

"Come and play a couple of tunes, Eva."

And Eva played "Karl Orsa's Polka" and "The Big Boot Waltz" and "The Floral Season Cometh" and "The Song of Kukumaffen," and whatever she played it sounded like a song of praise.

She was the daughter of Ol Karlsa who was Karl Orsa's father, so she was half sister to both Tilda and her father and also an aunt to her own sister and almost like a sister-in-law to her own mother. That's how things were.

□

To live without being guilty of debts is impossible, that's how you've made life, Lord. And the more we go at it and exert ourselves the larger the debt becomes, and what there is still to pay when we've done our utmost has to be left to your mercy and grace, but grace is a conditional and uncertain thing. Eva insisted on having a fiddle.

"I've got fiddle-playing hands," she said. "You can see, I was made for playing the fiddle."

And there was some truth in that: her long slender fingers seemed made for milking cows and playing the fiddle, they were darned strong and yet supple, she could bend them any way she wanted.

And Karl Orsa must have leered at her hands. Or else she'd held them out in front of him and said:

"Have you seen my playing fingers? My fiddle hands?"

He bought the fiddle in Skellefteå and hung it up in his shop so that everyone who thought they had fiddle hands would see it. It was streaky brown and shiny and the bow was there too and a little green box with the resin in it, and the fiddle hung in front of the harnesses and chains and fox traps and yokes and everything else that Karl Orsa had in the shop.

"Aren't you going to give the fiddle to Eva?" he said to Mother. "You've got the credit. Then you can play together. When she sees the fiddle she goes as stiff as an icicle and her eyes shine and she doesn't hear you speaking to her and she can stand there for hours. Don't be unreasonable, Thea."

"If only it had been something else," Mother said. "Anything else."

She meant: If only it hadn't been music. You can deny yourself anything, but not music.

So it was more or less forced on her.

Karl Orsa came over with the fiddle himself, he'd got hold of an oblong box for it and the bow was in the box too and there was a shiny string around the box, and Eva took the fiddle and she knew what to do straightaway. She'd already started to develop little titties, she put the fiddle between them and held it straight out in front of her and began tightening and plucking and tuning it—you really wouldn't have known it was the first fiddle she'd held—and then she took the bow and drew it carefully back and forth a few times across the strings, and then, believe it or not, she was playing.

And she really did have fiddle hands. Lord, how she played!

I don't remember what pieces she ran through, I don't even remember what it sounded like, I've never had a gift for music—but we were speechless and flabbergasted, Mother and I and Karl Orsa. She didn't need to learn the fiddle, she knew it all from birth—you, Lord, had even made the space between her breasts just fit the body of the fiddle.

But I do remember that she played "The Song of the

Lark." "Wild lark song will not last long when rain and storm o'erwhelm it."

And I remember that she bent over it so that her long shining hair touched the bow and her bowing hand, and Mother went behind her and lifted her hair up so that it wouldn't get in the way of the music and plaited it and tied it in a big knot on the top of her head, and it was as if Eva was completely alone with the fiddle, she didn't even notice when Mother put her hair up. Karl Orsa sat on the woodbin and leered at her—when he visited us he almost always sat on the woodbin—the fiddle wasn't paid for yet so it was as if he owned the music, he waggled his feet and looked at her, she was thirteen and Mother was over thirty, and the farmers around here have always been partial to music.

I would never have been able to hold the fiddle like Eva did, my chest is rounded and my breastbone sticks out like a chicken, due to rickets, the doctor says. She never changed in that respect, as long as she lived and was able to play she held the fiddle like that, between her breasts.

What it cost I don't know: if it ever had a price in sovereigns, it was never mentioned. For Mother the fiddle was more important than the price. Karl Orsa must have had some idea of what he wanted for it and it wasn't money, and you could hear straightaway that it was a valuable fiddle.

During the winter that Eva got the fiddle—I was sixteen then—I was at home with a pain in my chest, there was something there that I couldn't cough up. It came in the autumn and I got weak and miserable, I couldn't manage anything more than chopping some wood and shoveling a bit of snow and mending a few pairs of shoes. If Mother hadn't had her harmonium and credit and zest for life I don't know how it would have turned out. But we got through a day at a time and that's how things were and to whom shall we go, Lord? And in the evenings when it was dark Mother and Eva played; and I lay with my little sisters on the ancient bed and they played right through the hymnbook and dance music and the tunes they'd made up between them, I chewed resin for my chest and sucked cough drops, but the music seemed to soothe me more.

"We never need to light candles in the evenings," Mother would say, "because we have the music."

She was still so full of light within herself.

In '65 and '66 she bore two children to Karl Orsa, Father Unknown. A girl first, and she gave her away to a childless couple at Brännberg, and then a stillborn boy. He was premature and apparently had brown hair like Karl Orsa. She had him when she was playing at Kusträsk. In the middle of the night, after she'd finished playing, she suddenly felt ill when they were about to carry the harmonium out, and she gave birth to him on the floor of the hall where they'd been dancing. If he'd lived she would have called him Linus after the man who used to play the psalms for the apostle Paul in the Second Epistle to Timothy.

That was the last child she had.

Later in the autumn, that autumn, Jacob came back.

Our Lord had told him to return to us, that's what he claimed.

Was that really true?

He wasn't the same man anymore, not the same person at all. His beard was uncut and his clothes in tatters and he didn't even have a pair of skis to travel on and it was as if he'd come because he thought he had to. He was silent and downcast, he hardly showed any interest in Sarah and Rachel even though they were his. That first evening Mother was so glad to see him that she didn't realize he'd been through something that had changed him both outwardly and inwardly. She and Eva played for him and Mother talked to him without noticing that he wasn't answering, and in the evening she moved the beds and made them up again so that everything should be as it was before they came to fetch him.

The rent, she seemed to be thinking, and the credit and the repayments for the fiddle, now all those trials are over. And when these things begin to come to pass, then look up, and lift up your heads; for your redemption draweth nigh. And while she was tidying up and getting things ready for the night and clipping Jacob's beard she was singing softly and babbling to herself like a little girl.

And in a way all of us thought of Jacob as some kind of redeemer. The first morning after he came back I went off to see Karl Orsa. He was sitting in the parlor behind the shop and he didn't look up when I came in but I'm sure he saw me anyway.

"Jacob has come back," I said.

But Karl Orsa didn't say anything, he opened a book that was lying in front of him and leafed through it as if he was looking for a particular passage that he hadn't read.

"You remember Jacob?" I said. "The one you got them to take away?"

But it was as if he couldn't be bothered to wonder who this Jacob might be. And I felt myself becoming more and more arrogant and cocky.

"So from now on it will be nothing but cash," I said. "Remember that, Karl Orsa, nothing but money. And I'm going out to work too. So from now on."

Then he looked up and said:

"So he's some kind of miracle worker, this Jacob."

And just as I was about to answer, when he had at last started to speak, the coughing began. It was the worst coughing fit in my whole life, it came from deep inside my chest and it tore at the back of my breastbone like a hand with piercingly sharp nails. How long it lasted I don't know but I thought I was going to faint, it was as if my whole body was filled up with that cough. And at last I felt something give way inside my chest, something that came up through my throat and was the size of an egg so that my gullet was barely wide enough and when it was in my mouth the cough suddenly stopped and I spat it out in my hand. It was a black lump, absolutely round and hard. When I scratched it with a finger-nail it only made a little mark on the surface.

And from that moment on, after that coughing fit, I recovered completely and have never felt anything in my chest since.

Karl Orsa stood up and came over and looked at the lump in my hand. "Is it blood?" he said.

"I shouldn't think so," I said. "I've never coughed up any blood before."

"But it does look rather suspect," he said. "Clotted blood."

And then it was as if he wanted to remind me of my business:

"You shouldn't be going out to work yet awhile, boy. You shouldn't strain yourself. When you're coughing blood you ought to take it easy."

But I couldn't take my eyes off that black lump, everything stood still for me, I'd almost forgotten why I was there, it was as if I'd coughed away everything I'd planned, I couldn't do anything more, and in the end I went away without having settled matters with Karl Orsa. And perhaps that was just as well. I took the black lump home and Mother and Jacob couldn't work out what it was either.

Mother began to notice things and soon realized that Jacob wasn't himself any longer: there was no real sense in what he said, he talked a lot about what he was going to do but nothing came of it, he was going to this or that place to work but he never set off, and he took out his tools and things and other bits and pieces and intended to mend all sorts of things that were broken, but he just left them lying around, and for long hours he would sit absentmindedly and didn't hear her talking to him, it was as if he'd lost all his strength, and he never said a word about where they'd taken him that time when they fetched him and where he'd been all those years.

And he just couldn't do without the gin now. Karl Orsa supplied it for him. "I'll just saunter over to the shop," he would say casually, "my legs ache when I sit still like this. Is there anything you need, Thea?"

But she never did need anything, she had enough and to spare, and she knew perfectly well that a grown man couldn't just sit still doing nothing. "You go for a stroll, Jacob, I'm going to cook so there'll be a few cold potatoes for you."

When mother was thirty-five he gave her a shiny metal chain to wear around her neck.

And the gin made him so lively and good-humored that he asked Eva to play and he took Mother and danced with her; neither of them was a great dancer because Mother had always been providing the music and he didn't really have the talent for it, so their dancing was rather odd and clumsy and at the end they always fell over. And he talked to me in a way he didn't usually do, of all the things we were going to tackle by and by, a horse and another cow and the ditching and adding a few tiers of logs to make a bedroom in the loft and that it might be possible to buy our home back or that there were other places we could take over or that we could abandon this place, this damned marsh, and go off to Baggböle or Holmsund and work for a company and live on the money and not have any worries, for a company worker is like a lily of the field, and that for two real men by and by nothing would be impossible. It was as if you, Lord, gave us particular special grace and strength as we sat there in the evenings; Mother used to go to bed because she wasn't very interested in planning like that.

So that's how things were.

We didn't talk about the rent. The rent was only a small matter and he had some money anyway, and there was nothing special about Karl Orsa, he needn't imagine he was set up to rule like a petty king forever, not everyone would let the ground be taken from beneath his feet by a shopkeeper who'd never been farther than Skellefteå.

It was that winter that Karl Orsa changed his name to Markström. He wanted to have a real shopkeeper's name. But nobody took any notice of it, it was just entered in the parish register.

□

Lord, do you ever plan and dream the way Jacob and I did in the evenings when he'd had a drop to drink? We know it's all uncertain and yet we believe in it. Though you probably have no need to believe—the counsel of the Lord standeth forever, the thoughts of his heart to all generations. You have marked out all things from the beginning, every last detail, and we can talk and plan things out as much as we like, your judgments rule our every step.

Karl Orsa's steps were short and careful, he walked as if he was anxious to preserve some kind of dignity, almost like a churchwarden, he really believed his name was Markström.

We knew he would come but it was still a surprise to us. Mother and Eva had been playing at Cat Hill and had come home that morning, I sat carving a doll's head for Tilda, and Jacob was lying in bed with Mother and probably had a slight hangover. Karl Orsa was holding the almanac for '67 in his hand, and I thought, Jacob will get up now and bring out the money.

"So you haven't started the day yet," said Karl Orsa.

"We didn't know we were going to have an important visitor," said Mother.

Then Karl Orsa said:

"Love not sleep, lest thou come to poverty; open thine eyes, and thou shalt be satisfied with bread." He was well versed in the Bible.

"We haven't slept," said Mother. "We've been playing over at Cat Hill."

And he sat down on the woodbin while they got up and pulled on their clothes, he seemed to have plenty of time, he leaned against the wall near the stove and flipped back and forth through his almanac, the royal family and the movements of the heavenly bodies and the commonest animal ailments; the fiddle lay there on the table, Eva had wrapped it in a cloth and it seemed to me that it looked like a baby as it lay there; it still hadn't been paid for.

Jacob sat down on the stool by the door so that he almost looked like a visitor too and Mother opened the cellar hatch and took out a bottle of beer, Eva picked up the fiddle and put it away behind the bed, and I put a few billets on the stove. The little girls just sat and stared at Karl Orsa as they always did when we had visitors.

And I couldn't imagine where Jacob kept the money. Perhaps he kept it in the outhouse and that was the reason why he had to sit near the door. He was unpredictable, of course, he sat rubbing his blind eye, he had crumpled up, and looked like the spent egg sac of a perch, but perhaps he was still one of God's miracle workers. He didn't want the beer that Mother offered him.

"In Skellefteå they think things are going to get dearer," said Karl Orsa. "A darned sight dearer. No money's going to be enough."

"If you don't have any money you don't need to worry

about high prices," said Mother. "That's one advantage. When things are expensive it's worst for the ones who have money."

"You need cash for business," he said. "You can't stay in business without cash."

"Would you like some more beer?" Mother said.

He passed her his mug, and then he drank as if he was really thirsty.

"Where's Jacob?" said Mother.

And then I noticed that he wasn't sitting by the door any longer.

"He went out for a walk," I said. "His legs started aching."

I didn't want to say: he went to the outhouse to fetch the money that he'd put away. Jacob must have thought he would surprise us. He wanted to come to Karl Orsa like a thief in the night and take the ground from beneath his feet with the cash.

And you could see that Mother was suddenly looking preoccupied and thoughtful. Perhaps, after all . . . ?

"And how are things generally in Skellefteå?" she said in order to talk away the time it might take before Jacob came back.

"You know how things are in Skellefteå," said Karl Orsa. "A lot of business being done and very hectic. But I can't avoid it. Because of the shop."

Mother had never been as far as Skellefteå. She'd been to Norsjö for three funerals.

"Aye," she said, "that's how it is. Skellefteå. It's like Babylon."

And they talked for quite a while about Skellefteå, about people who had gone there and not come back and the tinkers who had fought with the farmers from Bure near the church there and the parson who had drowned himself in Ursvik Creek and how folk in the town tried to talk so fine that it was almost impossible to understand what they said. And

Mother said that if the smoked meat hadn't been eaten up she would have brought it out and he said that he really had already eaten and that smoked meat made him colicky. But no Jacob. He must have gone to the privy first, I thought. He wants us to give up hope. But then he'll come.

"But the worst thing is the money," said Karl Orsa. "It's as if it's never enough in Skellefteå."

And now Mother was pretty much at a loss.

"Aye," she said. "The money. It doesn't go far. That's how things are."

"So this rent of yours, Thea," he said. "It hasn't been put up since the old man died."

"Aye, that's true," said Mother.

"He was so kindhearted, the old man," said Karl Orsa. "He found it hard to charge people the right amount."

No, Jacob hadn't just gone straight to the privy. He didn't have any money in the outhouse. He didn't come back. At least not while there was still time.

"So we'll say three sovereigns more," said Karl Orsa. "I don't want to be unjust."

"It's up to you," said Mother. "But I haven't got any money, you know that."

And then she said:

"Johnny, you go out and see if you can find Jacob. And Eva, take Sarah and Rachel and Tilda out to the barn and mix up some bran for Angel."

But Jacob had hidden himself well. I went down through the whole village and ran halfway to Broadmere and shouted "Jacob!" into the forest, but no luck, he wasn't in the privy or in the shed, and it was so cold that the hasp on the outhouse door stuck to my hand. The same thing has happened to Jacob as happened to my father, I thought, he's gone mad. If he survives this and comes back they'll have to send him away to Pitholmen. Mother has darned bad luck with her men.

When I got home I saw that Karl Orsa hadn't gone yet, his dog-skin coat was lying against the windowpane, so I went to the barn and helped Eva make the bran for Angel.

After a while Mother came and said that he'd gone now and that it was strange of Jacob just to disappear like that, he wasn't dressed for the cold, and now we should go in and boil potatoes and Karl Orsa had had a piece of pork brawn in the pocket of his fur coat that we could have with them.

On the table lay the almanac for '67 and the pork brawn and a piece of cloth for Tilda and a sugarloaf.

In the evening after we'd gone to bed Jacob came back. He was so cold that he could barely walk. He sat down on the stool by the door where he'd sat before he went out and he didn't say a word, but Mother got up and took hold of him and led him to the bed and he lay down without taking off his clothes and in the end she managed to get some life back into him.

But in the morning when we woke up he'd gone again and Mother hadn't noticed him getting out of bed, but we said he's sure to come back because he can't stand the cold.

But by midday he still hadn't come. Then someone came over from the shop, one of Karl Orsa's servant girls, and said that Mother had to come, it was about Jacob.

When we got there the first thing we saw was Jacob. You couldn't help seeing him. He was sitting on top of the chimneystack of Karl Orsa's house, sitting quite still with his head in his hands looking neither up nor down. The people of the house were standing in the yard staring at him. Karl Orsa's house is huge and his chimneystack is higher than all the other chimneystacks, it was as if Jacob had tried to retreat as high up as possible, as if he'd been trying to reach the utmost point—Lord, to whom shall we go?

"Is that a gun he's got across his knees?" Mother asked.

"It's a muzzle loader," said Karl Orsa.

"He hasn't got a gun," said Mother.

"He came early this morning and wanted to buy it," said Karl Orsa. "And I gave it to him on credit. And a powder horn and black powder and fuses and a bag of shot."

"Is he going to shoot himself?" someone asked.

"He won't," said Mother.

And they started to say that he'd probably freeze to death, he didn't have enough clothes on and up there in the sky it was absolutely clear and cold, even colder than down on the ground where we were standing. But then Karl Orsa said that as long as they kept the stove burning there was no risk of that, Jacob was warmer than the rest of us, you could even see the wispy blue smoke behind his back from the birchwood and alderwood that they were burning. So no fear of that.

And some of us went up so close that we could only see his head above the roof, and we shouted to him to come to his senses, you heard us, Lord, we told him to throw away the gun and we'd give him the ladder that he'd kicked away and he could climb down, because it was totally pointless sitting up there on the chimneystack. Karl Orsa went in and brought out some gin and held it up and said he'd get a drink if he came down, and I shouted to him that by and by, and the horse that we'd get, and the little room in the loft, and the marshy patch behind the barn, and Baggböle and Holmsund . . . and a man from Kläppen who was a cousin of Karl Orsa and married to a half sister of Nicanor of Böle shouted that he ought to have pity on his children and come on down, for all little children need a father, he'd had mumps himself and hadn't had any children. But it was as if Jacob was deaf and blind, he didn't even shake his head, he just sat there absolutely still.

And of course folks living nearby heard that Thea's Jacob had climbed up onto Karl Orsa's chimneystack and that he was sitting there now with a gun and that anything might happen, no one knew how it would finish, for God's Creation is unending. So a lot of people came along to see Jacob, and they made a fire in the middle of the yard and stood there warming their hands and talking, and the crowd thought he'd simply gone mad and that he would presumably climb down eventually. And someone said it was probably Karl Orsa who'd hired him to do a crazy thing like that to get people to his shop. And someone knew that the same thing had happened to a man at Avaträsk, he went to sleep and fell down and was killed; people who sat on top of chimneystacks shouldn't be allowed to fall asleep.

But when they started saying that he might use the gun and that he could shoot dead anyone he wanted from up there, they got rather uneasy in the yard and several of them went inside the shop so as not to get shot. But then Mother said:

"He's no marksman. He's lost his aiming eye."

Some of them were invited in to eat at Karl Orsa's. They got roast meat, you could smell it when they opened the door.

And Jacob just sat where he was, you wouldn't have known that he usually got aches and pains from sitting still.

In the afternoon Karl Orsa hit on the idea of smoking him down with straw. And it really did give off horrible smoke, Jacob and the chimneystack disappeared completely, the smoke settled like a dense black cloud over the roof and we said: "Now, dammit!" But then a little gust of wind came and blew it all away and there he was again, still sitting there.

As evening came it began to snow, and when it got dark we went home. Karl Orsa set two men to look after the fire and keep a sort of watch. In the morning when it was light he wasn't sitting on the chimneystack anymore—how he'd managed to get down nobody knows, you couldn't see anything because of the fresh snow—and he'd stood the gun against the wall by the door.

That same day Karl Orsa came over with the gun.

"No one will want this gun," he said, "not after this. So I thought that you, Thea . . ."

"What do I want with a gun?" said Mother.

"Your boy. Johnny. At least he can shoot some squirrels."

"Isn't it a bit expensive?" Mother said.

"You've got credit, Thea," said Karl Orsa.

And I was pleased, of course. The snow was fresh, I tried it by shooting at a knot in the wall of the barn, I saw a hare down the hill but didn't have time to light the fuse, and I shot two squirrels just this side of Long Marsh.

□

And I must tell you about how Mother and Eva were paid for their playing: sometimes they got a shoulder of mutton or a piece of pork or a leg of veal, and sometimes they got cash. One of the dancers would go around with a cap just like taking a collection in church; they mostly got small coppers but sometimes a silver coin too. At the beginning of the week one of us took the money to Karl Orsa and he counted it and wrote it down in the book where the debts were recorded.

Jacob had had a page to himself in the book, Mother found that out after he'd disappeared. It was mostly gin, but also a pair of boots and a shiny metal necklace and four packets of snuff.

"I've crossed out his name and put yours instead, Thea," said Karl Orsa. "That's how it is with debts—someone has to take them over."

"You can have the necklace back again," said Mother. "And cross it out in the book."

"Necklaces don't sell," replied Karl Orsa. "Jacob was the only one. Nobody else wants them. That's the sort of man Jacob was."

And about the credit he said:

"Don't think you're the only one, Thea. Hardly anyone's free of debt. I even have big farmers in the book. A faithful man shall abound with blessings: but he that maketh haste to be rich shall not be innocent, so hardly anyone's free of debt."

"But you, Karl Orsa, don't have any debts," Mother remarked.

"Money debts," said Karl Orsa, "but they're a special kind."

And he went on:

"Not to mention interest. Even Jesus Christ said you should charge interest. That you were bad and lazy if you didn't make sure you received interest. If you owe a debt to the Lord then you have to make sure you receive his forgiveness now and then, and the interest on a money debt is like God's forgiveness for the fact that you can't repay it all at once."

"And when do you want the interest?" Mother said.

"For you I don't count the interest. I couldn't do that."

In the summer of '67 the potatoes froze in July and the spring had come so late that the barley didn't set ears till August and by then it was already frostbitten. In September we slaughtered the ewe, there was already snow then and by October the ice on the lake was thick enough to walk on. We wouldn't have survived that winter without your mercy, Lord, and Karl Orsa's credit, it was as if you and Karl Orsa had agreed to keep us alive; he said he came for the music and inside his dog-skin coat he carried potatoes and pieces of pork and flour and even sugar—he usually came once a week and made sure no one knew what he had in his coat, and each time he came we had to go out for a while and Mother paid off some of the debt. So while folk were starving everywhere else we managed reasonably well, I shot a hare now and then and we had dried fish and there was firewood so we didn't freeze.

Mother had only three engagements during the whole of that winter and those were funerals, they didn't want the fiddle, just the harmonium, they didn't think you could play funeral music on the fiddle, but she wasn't paid anything, you don't pay for funeral music.

But they were good times for Karl Orsa. In the spring he took over the whole of Böle village and half of Kläppen, five thousand acres of forest and ploughland and marshes and hay meadows, and how it happened I'm not quite sure, only that when the winter was over it was his. And by June he was the only man who had enough seed corn both for himself and to sell.

One day in the autumn of '67 as we sat eating Mother felt something sharp in her mouth and when she took it out it was a tooth, and she laughed and said it was really high time she lost her milk teeth. But after that a tooth fell out almost every day, and before Christmas she hadn't a single one left, the day she was thirty-six she lost her last tooth. And it was as if her face shriveled up and she became an old woman.

"Have you lost your teeth?" said Karl Orsa. "And you who were such a beauty."

How large the debt was when that winter was over I don't know, it must have been frightful, it can't still have been on a single page in Karl Orsa's book, perhaps he'd now opened a separate book just for us.

He came about the rent in the New Year, and from that day on I didn't understand you at all, Lord. It was so cold that the pedals had frozen on the harmonium so it couldn't be played and we sat around the stove to keep ourselves warm. But when Karl Orsa came Eva brought out the fiddle straightaway, as there was nothing wrong with that, and she put it between her tits and played, and we didn't talk because Karl Orsa wanted it to be that way, like King Saul he was refreshed by the music and was well. He sat with his hands stretched toward the stove and waggled his boots and leered at Eva.

When she stopped to rest her fingers for a moment he turned around to Mother and said:

"How old would she be now? Seventeen?"

"She's fifteen," Mother said. "But big for her age."

"You've suddenly aged, Thea," he said.

And Mother had to agree:

"Time passes no one by and no one gets any younger."

And she added:

"But you're in good shape, Karl Orsa."

And it was true, he was in good shape, he had filled out a bit and looked well fed, his hair was still black and glossy and his face was smooth apart from the furrows on the brow that he'd always had.

"Perhaps we ought to settle up," he said. "Our business."

"Shouldn't I get the beer?" Mother said. "And Eva has made up some new tunes that you haven't heard."

"I've thought a lot about you, Thea," he said. "You ought to give some things up. Your boy will soon be twenty. And your oldest girl's grown-up. So that you don't have so many worries."

"I've got nothing to give up," Mother said. "What should I give up?"

"You've got the debts, Thea. And the rent."

"That's how things are," Mother said. "And we do our best. None of us can do any more."

And then he said quite plainly what he was thinking:

"I want to settle things with Eva from now on. If Johnny can't get the money together. But it would be easiest to settle with Eva. And I'm not a wicked man."

When Mother realized what he meant she went as pale as death and stood up from her chair and was a little unsteady on her feet as if she was going to faint, and then she walked across the floor and lay down on the bed and nobody said a word.

Lord, to whom shall we go?

But then at last she sat up on the bed and said:

"Never. I'd rather you killed me, Karl Orsa."

"What pleasure would I get from killing you, Thea?" he said. "I don't want anything bad, I just want to settle things."

"My children aren't shop goods," she said. "My children aren't horseshoe nails and cotton cloth and twists of tobacco. And they're not money."

He was silent for a while. But then he said, and he sounded both pitiful and eager to get what he wanted:

"But I've taken a fancy to her. Do you understand that, Thea, I've taken a fancy to her."

And then Mother said—and she thought that would be the end of the matter:

"She's your half sister. Ol Karlsa was her father. You're her half brother.

"The nakedness of thy sister, the daughter of thy father, or daughter of thy mother, thou shalt not uncover," she went on. "For whosoever shall commit this abomination their souls shall be cut off from among their people."

But he wasn't a shopkeeper for nothing, he had thought the matter over and prepared himself:

"I've spoken to the parson," he said. "She has no father. 'Father unknown,' said the parson. So it can't be Ol Karlsa, he wasn't unknown."

And Mother fell silent. That's how things were. Answer not a fool according to his folly, lest thou also be like unto him. Karl Orsa was possessed, she wasn't going to argue with him.

"But if you don't want an arrangement, Thea," he said, "then debt recovery proceedings are all that's left. Justice has to take its course. Then there's nothing I can do."

"There's nothing here to take," Mother said.

"A sheep," said Karl Orsa. "And a cow for slaughter. And the harmonium. And the fiddle."

"You can take all of them," said Mother. "But you don't touch Eva."

Then he stood up and got ready to go, and when he had put on his fur coat he went up to Eva and took the fiddle out of her hands and put it under his arm, and as he stood in the doorway he said:

"Think it over again, Thea. For your own sake and for the children's."

When he'd gone there was utter silence, none of us knew what to do or what to say. Finally Mother said:

"The Lord can surely still perform miracles. And if you abandon hope you abandon everything."

And she took the sheep's tallow that I kept for the gun and greased the pedal mechanism in the harmonium so the pedals would move and then she started to play, and she didn't play hymns but dance music and happy tunes, and she even sang "The Song of Kukumaffen" for us, and it seemed a little easier to breathe and as if Karl Orsa didn't really have the power to do whatever he wanted with us. I've never been able to produce a single tune all my life, not so much as a verse of a hymn, you know that, Lord, but even so I wouldn't have been alive today if it hadn't been for music.

And Sarah and Rachel brought out the pinecones and made pigs and cows and goats on the floor for Tilda.

But when Mother had gone to the barn Eva put on her coat and went out, and I thought she was just going for a short walk so she didn't have to sit thinking about the fiddle and everything else. But when Mother came back from the barn she still hadn't returned.

And Mother had got things ready for the night and tucked Tilda in by the time she came, and when she did at last come she was carrying the fiddle under her arm and had the almanac for '68 in her hand.

Mother didn't say anything, she just went to the bed and lay down on her stomach and her whole body shook as if she was freezing to death, and when at last she sat up she was as old in the face as Grandmother was just before she died.

To whom shall we go?

But Eva sat down by the stove and went over the fiddle with her fingers as if to check that it wasn't damaged, and she turned the pegs and tuned it more carefully and exactly than she'd ever done before. Then she began to play, and it actually was possible to play funeral music on the fiddle after all: "Cankered by the worm unseen, Blooms will soon from cheeks be taken, And the fruit, though it be green, From the bough by wind is shaken."

☐

Lord, I've racked my brains a lot about Karl Orsa's bookkeeping. How did he set about deciding that one of our debts had been paid, how did he work it out? Everything has its price, and someone has to set the price, since the price isn't part of the world order, and how Karl Orsa went about it, I don't know, perhaps it was simply that his body was like a steelyard and a measuring rod. They say that in the beginning of time the human body was the only thing that could be used when something had to be measured. And with what measure ye mete, it shall be measured to you, are your own words, Lord, and that saying must have applied to Karl Orsa too.

Eva was very like Mother, they had the same fair glossy hair and they were both light of body and light of heart, you'd have said nothing was impossible for them, they were both nimble and they never had to think for long when something needed doing, it was as if their body and soul was one and the same thing.

For me it's always been as if my body has never quite kept up with my soul.

If Mother and Eva had been the same age they could have been sisters. But Mother soon got old, in both body and mind. When Karl Orsa decided he wanted Eva because she was somehow worth more than Mother it was a blow to Mother and she never got over it, never got over the fact that she wasn't good enough and that she couldn't protect Eva any longer. A month must have gone by without her touching the harmonium and she didn't seem to enjoy listening to Eva playing.

"And she's nothing but a child," she said.

Apart from that she didn't say anything, she was so quiet that it was a bit worrying, and she withdrew into herself so that it sometimes almost felt as if she was a stranger.

On Good Friday Karl Orsa arrived, and it was obvious that he'd come on some special kind of errand. He sat down on the woodbin and said nothing, but his eyes went over us as if he wanted to see whether we could bear to hear the reason for his visit, and he almost seemed a bit excited; Mother said nothing either and she never brought out the beer these days.

And finally, when he realized that we really were beginning to wonder why he'd come, he said it:

"Well—old Jacob. They've found him."

And there he paused for a moment, he wanted to make the most of his news and not get it over with all at once. Mother was standing by the table and it looked as if she wasn't paying any attention, but she was standing stock-still.

"They found him at Baggböle. Down by the river, in a pine tree."

And then he fell silent again, just as if he had to search his memory to recall what he knew.

"He'd hanged himself," he said at last. "With a bridle."

And then there was total silence, we didn't know what to do, that's how things were. Sarah and Rachel crept up on the bed and sat with their arms around one another, they did that sometimes, and I thought about Karl Orsa and tried to understand what he really wanted.

In the end Mother said, about Jacob:

"And he who was so afraid of everything."

That was all that was said, and what she really meant, I don't know.

And then Karl Orsa left, he had no other business with us that time, it was as if we'd somehow paid off a little bit of our debt just by being there to listen to what he had to say. He didn't say that he wanted Eva to go with him to the shop about the debts, that was what he used to do these days, he had always settled the accounts with Mother at our place, but he wanted Eva to come to the little parlor behind the shop.

There be three things which are too wonderful for me, yea, four which I know not: the way of an eagle in the air, the way of a serpent upon a rock, the way of a ship in the midst of the sea, and the way of a man with a maid.

In the summer of '68 Angel swelled up with bloat the first time she ate clover and we had to slaughter her. But we got a heifer on credit from Karl Orsa, she was called Taphath after a daughter of King Solomon, she was small and only had three teats but still turned out to be a good milker, though it was difficult to milk her because your fingers were always groping for the teat that wasn't there.

And that same summer the farmers at Risträsk and Heda built a frame saw by Stony Brook, it had two blades and an edger for trimming, they'd got relief payments for the year of famine and had some money left over and used it to build the saw. In the autumn Karl Orsa came and told Mother that there was something for Johnny to do now, really good earnings, and that he would talk to the Risträsk farmers, there was work for all sorts of people at a sawmill, he even knew of women who worked in the sawmills. And I said I was fit enough for work, if there was a job going, and it didn't have to be women's work, I was a grown man and a frame saw was nothing special.

And so I got a job as an assistant to the stackers, I stood on top of the stacks and laid out the sawn timber, and I got three crowns a week. But by October the sawing was finished and then it was felling in the forest; during the winter they had to cut the timber that was needed for sawing the next summer, and you earned less money in the forest.

And that was the last winter that Mother went out playing the harmonium. She'd begun to get some trouble in her fingers, and you know how it was, Lord, they went stiff and wouldn't serve her properly as they used to, she often sat holding them up in front of her and looking at them, but nothing showed on the outside.

"They won't obey me anymore," she said. "It's as if you can't talk to them."

She could still manage hymn tunes and dance music if it wasn't too fast, but a schottische or a fast polka was impossible; the dancers could hear things go wrong sometimes, and nothing is more important than the rhythm. So when they came over from Arnberg just before Christmas wanting music for a Saturday night they said they could get by with Eva and the fiddle, there weren't that many of them and it would be much simpler in a way and it couldn't be much fun for her, since she wasn't so young anymore, to have to be running backward and forward like a shuttle playing dance music.

"There's nothing I like better than playing the harmonium," Mother said.

"But still," said the dancers from Arnberg.

And then Mother realized that that's how things were,

her music wasn't even worth a few coins anymore, it wasn't worth the trouble of putting the harmonium on a sledge behind a horse, so she said no more and Eva went to play at Arnberg on her own.

She wanted me to go along when Eva went off to play. So if I was at home I did, it was something to do, anyway, although I wasn't a dancer, and anyone who tried to teach me soon gave up, and then I would sit beside Eva and listen to the music and fetch water for her when she was thirsty, and support her back when she got tired, and if I closed my eyes I hardly noticed them dancing and having a good time.

And Mother went on playing for herself, preferably when she was alone at home so that no one could hear her. "My fingers may recover again," she said. "Our Lord can do anything he wants, perhaps he intends my fingers not to move so quickly, religious music never goes quickly."

In April '69 I took the money that I'd earned that winter and went to Karl Orsa and laid it on his table in the little parlor behind the shop.

He looked at it thoughtfully for a moment, and then said: "What's this money for?"

"It's to pay off some of the debt," I said.

And then he thought for a while again.

"You should be careful with money," he said. "You shouldn't just chuck money away like that."

"I want you to write it down in the book," I said. "And deduct it from our debt."

He was always slow to speak, and now he was even slower than usual.

"No," he said. "It's not worth opening a book for that amount of money."

"It's as much as a year's rent," I said.

"Eva's already paid the rent," he said. "And don't worry yourself about the credit."

"You just take the money," I said. "And write it down in the book."

"I won't take it," he said. "And what I write in the book is no concern of yours."

And then I thought, I'm not arguing with him anymore, I'll never get to understand him, he moves like a serpent upon a rock, that's how he is, so I left the money lying on the table, said no more and went off, and he couldn't think of anything more to say either.

Some days later I was chopping up winter firewood on the slope above the farm fence, and when I came in one evening Mother said that Karl Orsa had called by and given Tilda a fistful of coins, and I saw the money and recognized it straightaway, and I told Mother that she shouldn't have accepted it. But he'd been so obstinate, she hadn't been able to give it back, he was pigheaded as well as everything else, and why he'd done it was a mystery to her.

"To think that you can even get money on credit," Mother said.

□

Mother was always so worried about Eva, it was as if she thought Eva had some kind of weakness, although she was so quick and hardworking and never ever complained about anything. Maybe it was because Eva was her eldest daughter and because she had all that music in her soul and in her hands, it was as if Mother thought Eva was more sensitive than an ordinary person. So she kept asking her whether she could feel pain anywhere and whether she was cold and whether she'd eaten enough and whether she'd slept as she should during the night, and after her own fingers had begun to stiffen she asked Eva several times a day whether she could feel anything strange in her fingers, and it sounded as if she expected what had happened to her to happen to Eva as well. And even when she didn't say anything you could see her turning things over in her mind, her eyes were worried and enquiring when she looked at Eva. After things had turned out as they had with Karl Orsa she always wanted to know about Eva's periods, whether they came when they should and whether they seemed the same as usual, and Eva probably never understood why Mother worried the way she did, she didn't have it in her to be afraid of anything evil, innocence shall guide the meek and whoever leads a blameless life shall live securely.

In the summer of '69 I was only at home for the haymaking and we moved no more than thirty hayracks in all. The rest of the time I was at the sawmill at Stony Brook, I was now earning four crowns a week and was called a stacker, though mostly I stood on top of the stacks taking the sawn timber from the stackers who were bigger than me. I took my wages home to Mother and what she did with the money I don't know, Karl Orsa wouldn't accept our money these days, so what use was it to us? He'd pushed us so far that he'd abolished money for us. Lord, what was your purpose in creating credit?

Mother was now thirty-eight, Eva was seventeen, Sarah fourteen and Rachel twelve, and I was twenty. Tilda was five. In August Karl Orsa found jobs for Sarah and Rachel in service, they needed to get away from home and do their bit, he said. Rachel was a little sad because she'd just started learning to play the harmonium. Sarah went to Aggträsk and Rachel to Björknäset.

That autumn Karl Orsa was ill for a while and got it into his head that he was going to die. It was inside his belly, a kind of lump behind his navel, he thought it was cancer and he even pulled up his shirt once to show us where it was, but there was nothing to see. While he went around dying like that he often came over to our place, for no particular reason—unless you'd call the cancer and music reasons of a sort. He would sit there in silence on the woodbin and would want Mother to play for him even though it sounded the way it did. Eva was left in peace at that time except that he wanted her to play the fiddle for him, "Now my hours of life declining, Move toward their peaceful goal."

And Mother told him he ought to get some tansy that was in flower then and dry the blossoms and eat them, and put them in his gin too, so that if he made sure he drank a lot and peed a lot it would probably do some good—she knew they'd done that in the old days and that it was like a miracle cure—and he could keep the blossoms in a bag and let them lie on his belly at night when he slept.

"I can't sleep at nights," was his response to that, and he sounded miserable.

"That may well be for reasons other than your belly," said Mother.

To which he replied:

"It'll be my cousin's children at Gallejaur who'll inherit it all from me. And they don't understand a thing about business."

And:

"I'll tear your debt out of the book, Thea. When I'm gone you'll be as free of debt as a newborn babe."

And he seemed even better versed in the Bible than usual:

"Take no thought for your life," he said, "what ye shall eat, nor yet for your body, what ye shall put on. Life is more than meat, and the body more than raiment."

Mother should never have told him about tansy. It must have been the dried blossoms that made him well. I can't believe that you, Lord, performed a miracle with Karl Orsa.

Though who can fathom him who is wise and mighty and removeth mountains and they know not and shaketh the earth out of her place, and the pillars thereof tremble?

He stayed away for a while and then he came and said he wanted Eva to go with him to the shop again, there was still a lot to be sorted out and settled, and what had happened to the lump behind his navel we never found out, and Mother said that of all people on earth whoremongers live the longest.

They got a new servant girl at Karl Orsa's that autumn, she was called Johanna, and I went over there to have a look at her when she first arrived. She was small and thin with yellowish brown hair, but she had big tits and her eyes were quick and sort of restless, she came from Åmsele.

And she was easy to talk to, we soon got acquainted, she called me Johan and nobody else has ever done that. When she heard that we'd got a harmonium and a fiddle she said she'd come and see us when she had time, for music was the only thing that made her really feel like a human being, she had an uncle at Mårdsele who had a harmonium and she'd played on it when she was little.

What is man, that thou shouldest magnify him and that thou shouldest set thine heart upon him? And that thou shouldest visit him every morning, and try him every moment? That Johanna was like a revelation to me, if they hadn't come and sent her down to the cellar to fetch turnips I could have stayed there all day talking to her. And then she came over on Sundays, when she was given some time off in the afternoon, and she and Eva soon became friends. She could play too, and Mother taught her everything she didn't already know and after only a month it sounded as if she'd never done anything else than play the harmonium. So when they came from Brinkliden and wanted Eva to come and play Eva said she wanted to take Johanna and the harmonium with her, and the farmers' lads from Brinkliden said that would be all right as long as there was no extra charge, the farmers in this area have always been partial to music. And that's how it was from then on, they played together, and Karl Orsa said he didn't interfere in what his servant girls got up to as long as they didn't lead an immoral life.

And Mother scrutinized Eva regularly night and morning to see if anything had happened to her, and I know for a fact that she constantly spoke to you, Lord, about her not getting in the family way, for she was sure neither you nor she could stand that, and she tried to talk to Karl Orsa but he showed no compassion. "When it's a matter of business," he said, "you can't be lenient or sensitive." But Eva seemed to tell herself that that's how things were and that if thine enemy be hungry, give him bread to eat; and if he be thirsty, give him water to drink; for thou shalt heap coals of fire upon his head. It was as if she'd been born just for that: to play the fiddle and to take care of our debts.

And eventually Mother almost began to believe she was barren.

Actually we never talked about what was unavoidable— why talk and argue about things you can't prevent?

□

I'll tell you all of it just as it was.

After New Year in 1870 I went to Baggböle and got a job there as a stacker, though Lindström, who was in charge of the timber yard, thought I was on the small side. On the 9th of March, Forty Martyrs' Day, I fell down from a stack, I fell headfirst and the pad I was wearing on my left shoulder took the brunt of it, but I broke a bone in my chest so I couldn't move my arm. I got a lift with a carter from Lycksele, and got off the wagon at Åmsele and found out where Johanna's house was. Her father was working at Betsele, but her mother was at home—she was incredibly fat—sitting by the stove cutting up dried fish for the dogs.

"Johanna comes to our place a lot," I said. "She plays the harmonium."

"She's always been mad on music," she said. "But we hope she'll turn out decent and respectable."

"The harmonium is mostly used for playing hymns," I said.

"We all know what it's like with music," she said. "Maybe it's all right for them that sing a hymn now and again. But them that play . . ."

"My mother's played all her life," I said.

"I don't know her," said Johanna's mother. "So I couldn't say."

"A lot of folk find a kind of happiness in music," I said. "Mother's always comforted herself with music."

"But how've things turned out for her?" said Johanna's mother. "How's she got on in life?"

I said no more after that, we could have argued endlessly about music, the dogs were fighting over the dried fish, she didn't ask about Johanna and she didn't even ask who I was or where I came from, nor did she notice that my left arm was hanging straight down like the weight in a clock, and I was hungry but she didn't bring out so much as a crust of bread. So after a while I left without us having become better acquainted, the dogs followed me to the door and barked—they were elkhounds, Johanna's father used to hunt elk. I stopped over with a farming couple at Ajaur for the night and they gave me some barley porridge.

The bone in my chest didn't mend again until that summer, I went around the whole spring without being able to do a thing, at first I couldn't even hunt, and mostly I sat talking to Mother or went across to the shop now and then—Johanna had to help out there a lot because Karl Orsa was always buying in more and more of everything, so one of the servant girls had to be in the shop all the time.

"You're here in the shop a lot," Karl Orsa said to me once. "You shouldn't strain your credit."

"I'm not buying anything," I said. "I'm just looking around."

"That can be costly too," he said. "Looking around."

"Do you want to drive your customers away?" I said.

"You shouldn't be so touchy," he answered, because he saw I was riled. "You've got to learn to take a bit of teasing, Johnny."

And then he took out half a sugarloaf and told me to take it home for Tilda. Lord, thou who searchest all hearts and understandeth all the imaginations of the thoughts, did you ever understand Karl Orsa?

While I was going around being useless with that arm of mine, in the spring of '70, Johanna told me one Sunday evening that they'd moved her to the little room behind the kitchen and that she was alone there at night. So I went and stood outside in the yard behind the big mountain ash waiting till I saw they'd blown out the last candle at Karl Orsa's—and I didn't have to wait long because they always went to bed early to save the tallow and candle grease—and then I went in to Johanna. She'd already undressed and gone to bed. I remember she laughed at me when I said that the worst thing was that arm of mine that made me less of a man than I would have been normally.

She was the first woman I lay with. And the only one.

Mother realized straightaway how things were between me and Johanna. And she tried to tell me what I should do to make things go all right so I wouldn't get Johanna in the family way, to be as careful as when you're carving the handle on a cup, though it was pretty much too late by then anyway.

And Eva wasn't barren. Just before Easter Mother was quite sure, she knew all the signs and she could never be mistaken, and then she was so heartbroken that she didn't get up for two days. But on the third day, when Eva came in from the barn after milking Taphath, she got up and dressed and put a black shawl over her hair and went over to Karl Orsa. He said they could go into the parlor if there was something to be discussed.

"So that's how things are," Mother said. "With Eva."

But he didn't seem to understand.

"She was quite fit and lively when I last saw her," he said.

"She must be in her third month," said Mother. "You had her over here the last Saturday before Lent. That's when it happened."

"I only talked to her," said Karl Orsa. "We talked about your debts, Thea. And I gave her a piece of cloth for an apron."

"I can take you to court, Karl Orsa," said Mother.

"Better not," he said. "With your debts. And I can take an oath. But you can never take an oath about your debts. And who would keep you then?"

"Johnny will soon be fit," Mother said. "His arm has nearly mended."

"He's got enough troubles of his own," said Karl Orsa. "And even with two arms he's hardly a Samson."

"A father must take responsibility for his children," Mother said. "That's a duty before our Lord."

"And who would believe you, Thea?" said Karl Orsa. "You who've had six bastards yourself. And Eva going out playing at dances?"

"If you were as careful with your cock as you are with everything else this would never have happened," Mother said.

"I haven't got any debts," he said. "I run the shop carefully so that I'll never get into debt."

"Eva is your sister," said Mother. "And it is written that thou shalt not uncover the nakedness of thy father's daughter or the nakedness of thy mother's daughter."

"I've spoken to the parson," said Karl Orsa. "I'm not related to Eva in any way."

"You shouldn't have asked the parson," said Mother. "You should have asked Ol Karlsa, your father, while he was alive."

"He handed over everything to me," said Karl Orsa. "And he didn't say a word about any child."

"Eva's child will have his uncle, the brother of his own mother, for a father," said Mother. "And he'll be a brother of his mother's sisters. And Eva will be his aunt as well as his mother. And he'll be his own cousin."

"It won't be a boy," said Karl Orsa. "Bastards are hardly ever boys."

"You'll be her uncle and her father," said Mother. "And you know what inbreeding means. Have you thought about that?"

And now he really did think about it, it was as if he did finally take in a little bit of what Mother had said.

"It is written," he said at last, "that if any man will sue thee at the law, and take away thy coat, let him have thy cloak also. So I'll delete what's in the book, Thea. I'll mark it down that the fiddle is fully paid for. And the heifer. Not because I owe you anything, but for the love of our Lord."

"And nothing else?" said Mother.

"That's already going a lot further than what's really a sensible deal," he said.

"How will you be able to answer for this?" said Mother.

"As long as your books are in order," said Karl Orsa, "you have nothing to fear on the day of reckoning."

And then they both fell silent, it was as if it was hard to think of anything else to say. But in the end Karl Orsa said:

"Your boy Johnny has got one of my servant girls in the family way. You haven't got your children under very good control, Thea."

And Mother said nothing.

"He doesn't look like a whoremonger," said Karl Orsa. "But even so."

And what could Mother have said?

"I don't want my servant girls to have bastards," he went on. "It's not good for business. People talk something terrible."

"So people's gossip is your only yardstick, is it?" said Mother.

"But I've been thinking about it," he said. "They may need help. And I'm not one to bear a grudge."

"What am I to do?" was the only thing Mother could think of saying. "What am I to do?"

"If you send Johnny over here I'll talk to him," said Karl Orsa. "We'll arrange for everything to be done right and proper. As it should be."

And Mother had given up completely. To whom shall we go?

So she just turned and left the parlor and walked out through the shop, she'd taken off her black shawl since she no longer cared if anyone saw that her hair was gray, and Karl Orsa followed her. When they got to the door she finally recovered herself and said:

"You're unnatural. You're like the way of a serpent upon a rock."

"I don't want my house to be a den of vice," said Karl Orsa. "That's all."

So later that evening I went to Karl Orsa and he told me and Johanna how everything would be arranged, we'd get a ride with a load of barley flour to Norsjö and ask for the banns to be published and then we'd get married in the parsonage when the period of notice was over, and I could have his black suit which he didn't use anymore and Johanna could wear the Sunday dress that she wore when she was playing at dances. He knew exactly what we had to do, although he wasn't married himself and had no intention whatever of being crazy enough to get married, and we could have the rings on credit. And I was quite flabbergasted, we are troubled on every side, yet not distressed, we are perplexed, but not in despair, persecuted, but not forsaken, cast down, but not destroyed, and my bad arm was still hanging down like the weight in a clock.

□

I exercised my left arm again by walking in the forest with my gun. If I had to act fast when a hare or a squirrel appeared in front of me my arm forgot it was injured and did everything almost as it should, it was the gun that healed my arm, and I shot enough small game for Karl Orsa to value their pelts at ten crowns.

Johanna had to leave Karl Orsa's and she moved in with us. Rachel and Sarah's bed was still there and one extra mouth to feed made no difference, we had credit, and Eva and Johanna said the babes they were carrying would be like brother and sister. And they pressed each other's bellies and felt the unborn infants kicking against their hands.

Eva grew absurdly big and she ate as much as two grown men, but Johanna only got a little bit rounder, as if she was putting on some weight, that's all.

When we'd finished with the hay and I'd chopped the wood for the winter I got a job at the sawmill by Stony Brook. That lasted into October.

On the 27th of October Johanna's time came. Mother helped her and everything went quickly and smoothly as if she'd already had a lot of children. It was a girl and Johanna wanted her to be called Sabina because it was the name day she was born on. Karl Orsa gave her a china plate that had SOPHIA written on it, she was the crown princess.

But things didn't go so well for Eva.

Lord, nobody's books are in such good order as yours,
nothing is ever crossed out. If grace exists you keep it to
yourself and well hidden, I don't understand it. It is written
that God resisteth the proud, and giveth grace to the humble.
Should Eva have been even more humble than she was? Perhaps it was her music that wasn't humble enough? When she
was confined she wanted to have the fiddle on her belly, she
couldn't use the bow of course, but she lay plucking it with
her fingers so that you could still make out the tunes she was
thinking, For life's short span of pain and mirth I cannot be
intended, Not just a worm to creep on earth, Its progress there
soon ended. And, In a field the maiden turned hay with her
rake, "Gladly," the swain said, "I'd die for your sake."

When her pains began I took Tilda and went out to the
barn. I had a piece of charcoal and wrote letters on the logs
for her to learn, she was six years old and a really fast learner.
When we'd written all the letters and all our names and I
couldn't think what else to do, Mother came and said that
things weren't going as they should with Eva, nothing was
happening, I was to go at once and fetch Erik's Hannah, who
was the one usually called for at births.

So that's what I did, and Tilda was left alone with
Taphath in the barn. Hannah said she'd had a feeling someone would be needing her, she said that to everyone who came,
she just sat by the window doing nothing.

Eva was lying in bed when we got there, not moving,
and she paid no attention to us, she was enormous, it was the
first time I'd seen a woman in labor. Johanna was sitting on
the woodbin giving suck to Sabina, I remember it so well.

And Erik's Hannah went up to her and squeezed her belly
and laid her cheek against it to see if she could hear anything,
and she didn't notice me still being there. And she opened her
slit as if she could look right inside her body, and she squeezed

and slapped the outside of her belly over and over again and
laid her cheek against it. Then finally she said:

"There's no life in that one. It'll be stillborn. And the size
of two newborn babies."

Nothing showed in Mother's face, hardly anything ever
showed these days, they stood quite still and looked at Eva,
both Mother and Erik's Hannah. But at last Mother said:

"Are you sure there's no life there?"

That was the first thing she thought of: life.

"It's as dead as a stone."

And only then did Mother speak of Eva:

"Will she be able to give birth to it?"

"Not without help," said Erik's Hannah. "If then even."

And she said she wanted soap or sheep's tallow for her
hands so that she wouldn't hurt Eva more than necessary. I
went out to the barn to Tilda, Taphath had settled down and
Tilda was lying against her stomach asleep, I sat down beside
her and I think I could hear Eva all the way out there. When
Mother came I'd fallen asleep too.

"It's all over now," she said. "You can come back in."

Eva was sleeping. She had shrunk and was thinner and
whiter than ever before—while she was carrying the child we
hadn't seen how terribly skinny she'd got, big and skinny, she
looked as if she'd never wake up again. Lord, to whom shall
we go?

The dead baby was lying at the foot of the bed.

"It's a boy," said Mother.

He was as big as babies usually are when they start
learning to walk and his eyes were closed as if he was asleep,
he didn't seem to have suffered any pain but looked almost
contented, he was so fat that his skin glistened and his fingers
were spread because they were so fat and his cheeks were as
round as if he'd got something big and tasty in his mouth, a

sugarloaf. And Erik's Hannah explained to us what it was we could see:

"He's eaten her away like a wild beast, he's eaten like someone with no limit to his stomach and then he's died, he's eaten himself to death, he's eaten and drunk until he had a stroke. He's sucked the life out of her."

And then after a while:

"What kind of person would he have become?"

And finally:

"Who might his father be?"

"That's a matter between Eva and our Lord," said Mother.

But of course she was thinking, He's Karl Orsa's boy, he was like his father by nature, it was a mercy of our Lord to let him die, he was the kind that sucks life and blood.

But I'm sure she didn't think what I was thinking, Lord, why did you ever bother to create him?

After Erik's Hannah had gone Mother and Johanna helped one another to wrap the baby in an old sheet, leaving his face uncovered, and they laid him on two floorboards that I brought in and set up between two chairs. And Eva slept so you could hardly see she was breathing.

"Now we have to get Karl Orsa over here," said Mother. "He's got a right to see his child."

"It's evening," I said. "They'll have gone to bed at Karl Orsa's."

"Then we'll have to wake him up," Mother said.

"He'll be in a pretty foul mood if he's not left in peace at night," I said.

"If you won't go I'll go myself," Mother said.

So I went. It was dark at Karl Orsa's but I knocked on the door with a stone and the new servant girl came out, the one who'd replaced Johanna, and I told her to fetch Karl Orsa.

"I wouldn't dare to," she said. "You'll have to do it yourself."

So I went up the stairs and opened his door and said:

"Karl Orsa. Mother says you're to come over to our place."

And I thought, Now he'll kill me.

But he just got up immediately, he didn't say a word, not even to ask what it was Mother wanted, he pulled on his trousers and his shirt and a knitted pullover and the dog-skin coat that hung by the door and then he came, and he was in such a hurry that he almost pushed me over on the stairs, and when we got outside he half ran up the road, it had been snowing during the evening so it wasn't totally dark.

When we came in Mother and Johanna were sitting by the table, they'd put Tilda to bed and Eva was asleep, she hadn't moved, and although the light was dim he saw the stillborn child straightaway.

"That's your boy," Mother said.

"So he never lived?" said Karl Orsa.

"He was already dead when her waters broke," Mother said.

And he took the candle that was standing on the table and went up to the dead baby boy and leaned forward and shone the light on his face and stood there for quite a while saying nothing, and Mother claimed afterward that his eyes turned moist and he had to wipe his face with the back of his hand.

At last he said:

"And he was big and handsome."

"He was too greedy, he ate himself to death in the womb," said Mother.

"But a fine boy," said Karl Orsa.

"He was unnatural," said Mother. "He almost sucked the life out of Eva through the navel cord."

And then it was as if Karl Orsa remembered about her at last.

"She must be completely done in after this," he said.

"She's sleeping," said Mother. "She's sleeping as if she never meant to wake up again."

"But she's got her zest for life," he said.

And he put the candle back on the table and stood where he was and seemed at a loss what to do, and Mother sat examining her fingers, they were quite stiff now and there were small lumps on them and they nearly always ached. In the end she said:

"What do you want us to do with him?"

And then I said, because I wanted to put an end to all this:

"Stillborn babies are usually just buried. They don't need a funeral service."

"But he doesn't look like a stillborn baby," said Mother. "He looks like a fully formed human being."

"I can take him," said Karl Orsa. "If I can do you that little service, Thea."

"You do as you wish," Mother said. "It says in the Scriptures that the Lord shall turn the heart of the fathers to the children. So take your child, Karl Orsa. If anyone's got a right to it it's you."

And so Karl Orsa took the boy in his arms, he carried him as if he was an ordinary baby, and Johanna got up and opened the door for him so that he could get out, and what he did with him afterward I don't know, we never asked, a stillborn child is like a stranger, not even Tilda asked about him the next morning.

Eva didn't wake up in the morning, and when Johanna lifted the rug we saw there was a lot of blood in the bed.

So I went straight over and fetched Erik's Hannah again.

"I had a feeling someone would be needing me," she said.

And when she'd examined Eva and looked at everything there was to see she said that that's how things were.

"The stillborn baby was too big," she said. "It's ripped her apart inside. It's torn the arteries in the womb. She'll soon have no blood left."

"So she won't pull through?" Mother said.

"She might if the Lord performed a miracle with her," said Erik's Hannah.

Lord, you were with us all the time through all those days, why did you just look on, why didn't you stretch forth your omnipotent hand to help Eva? The eyes of the Lord are in every place, beholding the evil and the good, but why do you content yourself with beholding? Except for the times when you really turn everything upside down?

"So you don't know what to do?" said Mother.

"If you've got any mustard," said Erik's Hannah, "you can rub it over her belly. But otherwise . . ."

"So there's nothing else?" said Mother.

"No. Nothing else."

So I ran to the shop and got the mustard, and Johanna smeared it over her belly, and Mother sat by the table and kept her eyes closed and didn't move, it was as if she was unconscious, although she was sitting upright, when we spoke to her she didn't hear us, and Eva went on breathing, though slowly, until the afternoon, and then it was over.

She was eighteen years old.

When Johanna saw she was dead it was as if she herself was finished, she took Sabina and huddled up with her in our bed and turned toward the wall and lay quite still. But Mother seemed to wake up, she opened her eyes and looked at me and said:

"Now Karl Orsa has to be fetched."

"Do we really have to?" I said.

"We have to," she said.

So I went and got him.

I didn't say a word about how things were with Eva, but it was as if he knew it.

He went straight up to her bed, he didn't say anything, and he went down on his knees and lowered his head so that his face lay against her long hair, and how long he lay like that I don't know, and now and then his whole body quivered as if someone had taken hold of him and lifted him up and shaken him, and Mother sat quite still looking at him and saying nothing.

When he finally stood up his face was red and kind of swollen, and he didn't look at any of us.

In the doorway he turned around and said:

"I'll take care of everything."

That was the only thing that was said. And however strange it may sound it was like a real help and comfort to hear it: that Karl Orsa would take care of everything.

□

And he really did take care of everything—he got a coffin and he took Eva to Norsjö, Mother and I followed behind on a cartload of oats, Johanna stayed at home with Tilda and Sabina, there were three horses in the funeral procession, the last of the loads was a pig's carcass and bundle of sheepskins that Karl Orsa was going to give to the parson and the church.

The parson spoke of thee, Lord, who hast mercy on whom thou wilt have mercy, and whom thou wilt thou hardenest.

Karl Orsa asked Mother to travel beside him on the way back from Norsjö. It felt as if he was part of the house of mourning he said, and he told her he'd crossed off all our debts in the book now, he'd let us off everything, we were as free from debt as newborn babes.

But Mother couldn't bring herself to thank him.

Mother never recovered after Eva's death. Her fingers got stiffer and stiffer and lumps appeared on her ankles and knees, but it was as if she didn't care about it. Johanna saw to the things that needed doing and Tilda was good at helping, so Mother mostly sat at the table reading the Bible and when she thought she was alone she talked to herself.

In the New Year of '71 Karl Orsa came over and said that he wouldn't take any rent that year, we'd get a free year, he'd been thinking a lot about us, and we got the almanac anyway. As he was about to go he said:

"Nobody plays the fiddle now, I suppose?"

"No," I said. "But I've thought of hanging it on the wall. It would be a sort of decoration."

But then Karl Orsa said he thought he had a buyer from Risliden, and when he left he took the fiddle under his arm, and Tilda started to cry because she seemed to think she'd inherit the fiddle, though she hadn't any talent for music.

In March I went to Baggböle and got a job there straightaway, Lindström remembered me very well. During the summer I only went home for the haymaking, and when I finished in November I had enough money for the rent and more. Just before Christmas, on the 17th of December, Johanna had a girl; we christened her Eva after her aunt.

After Epiphany Mother didn't get up.

"Why should I get up?" she said. "It's easier for me to lie here, and there's no point in wearing out clothes unnecessarily."

She was forty then, I was twenty-two, Tilda was seven, Sabina was one year old and had just learned to walk, and Eva was newborn.

And Mother couldn't stand music any longer. When Johanna sat down and played she said:

"I get a pain behind my eyes from music. You can play when I'm asleep."

So Johanna played the harmonium in the evenings when Mother had fallen asleep, though sometimes she woke up and said she was having such bad dreams and that it was probably because of the music, but she never told us what she'd dreamed.

Johanna worked hard, she looked after the barn and the little ones and Mother and never complained. You know she never complained. She used to sing to herself, it was a sort of habit and she didn't know she was singing. "The splendor of the roses my heart to joy disposes, Whenever I stroll around the rose garden fair."

I tried once to talk to Mother about whether it might be an illness she had. But she just said that that's how things were, it might be some kind of weakness but nothing happens unless it's the will of the Lord.

But to this day I don't know who it was wanted her to die, whether it was herself or you, Lord.

She lived until the beginning of the summer. But on the second Sunday in June when we woke up she was dead. And I remember we sat down at the table when Johanna came in from the barn and I opened the Book and read the text for that day: Every branch in me that beareth not fruit he taketh away, and every branch that beareth fruit he purgeth it, that it may bring forth more fruit. Now ye are clean through the word which I have spoken unto you.

In the autumn, the day before I was due to leave for Baggböle, Karl Orsa came and said he'd decided to take care of Tilda.

"She's like an orphan now," he said. "And I'll never have any children of my own."

"Can I be in the shop, then?" said Tilda.

Sugarloaves, she thought.

"She'd be like a foster child," said Karl Orsa. "Not just living in."

"I think of her as a little sister," said Johanna.

But she probably said that mainly because she felt she had to, Tilda wasn't like either Mother or Eva, she was most like Karl Orsa, she was calculating and shrewd and she had dark hair and brown eyes.

"I don't know," I said to Karl Orsa.

"This isn't a business matter," he said. "I'm not going to pay to take her."

"It's not that," I said. "I'm man enough to support my family, that I can tell you."

"It's only meant as a suggestion," said Karl Orsa. "An offer. That's all."

"She should be allowed to do what she wants herself," I said. "We shouldn't arrange things too much for children. We don't own their lives."

I was almost sure she would want to stay with Johanna, they were nearly always together and Johanna was amazingly patient with her.

"I want to be in the shop with Karl Orsa," she said.

And it made no difference that we tried to talk to her, she just looked straight ahead and didn't answer us, and she even went up to Karl Orsa as he stood by the woodbin and took him by the hand, and it did look rather odd, he'd probably never held a small child by the hand before.

And she was in such a hurry that she didn't want to take anything with her, not her clothes nor even the doll that I'd made the body and the head of and Johanna had sewn the clothes for—she was like an old person who's finally decided to start a new life, there was nothing at our place that she wanted to take along with her, she wanted to go at once and Karl Orsa said she could have the little room behind the kitchen all to herself.

Karl Orsa's Tilda. Everything must have a name.

So when I went to Baggböle there was only Johanna and Sabina and Eva left, and it felt emptiest of all because of Mother.

□

Mother was not an ordinary person.

She seemed to tie her own life up with our lives so that she was inside us all the time, even if she wasn't anywhere near it was as if she was beside us, and she still hasn't entirely faded away.

She always kept track of time like no one else, not that she always knew what time of day or what day it was, but in the sense that she was always aware of what had already happened and was done with forever and what was taking place right now and what hadn't yet happened, things that were in the future and weren't to be worried about—she never talked about my father because he belonged to the past.

Except toward the end, when she abandoned time altogether.

She said then that she would have liked to remember what he looked like, but she couldn't.

She had such a light and sunny nature. However many debts she incurred, her soul remained free of them all. She couldn't be affected within, there is nothing from without a man, that entering into him can defile him, but the things which come out of him, those are they that defile the man. When I was little and there wasn't enough food she would play the harmonium for us: "Lord! You graciously us spare, Of your bounty each a share, Food and drink to us you give, That we all refreshed may live."

She was strong, she was stronger than Karl Orsa, he never really had any power over her.

□

Karl Orsa's Tilda, when she was little she was my half sister, but after she moved away from us we weren't related anymore. In the autumn of '73 when Karl Orsa was fifty and Tilda was nine, she decided they should have a big party for Karl Orsa, the main customers and relatives from Granliden and Kvavisberg and Gallejaur, and she sent the farmhands over to us to fetch Johanna and the harmonium.

She herself wore a new frock from Skellefteå.

And she didn't know Johanna, she'd written on a piece of paper what tunes were to be played and she arranged that Johanna should be given beer and a chicken breast while the parson made his speech, and when the party was over she made sure that three crowns were paid for the music, but she said not a word to Johanna herself, she didn't know her.

For what man knoweth the things of a man?

I was at the sawmill at Baggböle for two years, I only went home for the haymaking and for a while in the middle of winter when they weren't sawing every day, and the earnings were enough for me to pay the rent and whatever Johanna had taken on credit while I was away.

A stacker should be able to carry three two-inch planks on his shoulder. On the 20th of November '74, just before noon, I was carrying six two-inch planks on my shoulder—a man from Bratten called Alexi had carried five before me so the whole thing was his fault. Halfway up I had to move my left hand and my right foot slipped and something snapped in my back—the men behind me must have heard the crack, though they say they didn't hear anything—something broke in my back just below the shoulder blades and I had to drop all six of the two-inch planks.

That's how things were.

And I couldn't lift my arms, they just hung there.

And I told Alexi from Bratten:

"It's your fault. It was you who made me break my back."

So come New Year of '75 we had no money.

And Karl Orsa knew it.

"I'll settle up with Johanna," he said.

"You won't," I said. "Not as long as I live."

"You can play a piece for me, Johanna," he said.

And Johanna didn't have any choice, I went out and stood on the steps while she played, because I got a sort of pain in my chest from the music, it was so cold that I could see my hands turning white as I stood there, and I didn't go in until the harmonium stopped. But it was as if he didn't need anything more than the music on that particular day, he already had his dog-skin coat on.

"Our Lord has said that we should be forbearing," he said as he left. "Though justice has to take its course."

And when he came again the next day he didn't ask for music. "Debt recovery proceedings," he said. "If we can't settle up in a friendly manner. For those who do what the law demands shall be regarded as righteous. So there."

And the third time he just said he'd be going to Skellefteå the next day.

"If there was anything I could do," he said. "But the law is the law. And as you aren't willing to settle up in a friendly manner . . ."

Then I was completely at a loss and didn't know what to do, in the evening I went to the barn. And there I sat talking to you, Lord.

"If I can't bring my questions to you I'm done for," I said.

And then I asked about everything.

When I came back in Johanna wasn't there, I could see right away how things were, there was nothing else she could do, and I told myself that when people have no choice they might do almost anything, and that was a kind of comfort.

When she came back she didn't say anything, we didn't talk about it that night, that's how things were, I followed her when she went to milk Taphath. Lord, to whom shall we go?

The following weekend he brought the almanac.

"And credit," he said. "If you need it you've got credit, Johnny. In case you run short of anything."

It seemed a matter of course to him, but to me it was a taunt, I didn't understand business. It felt as if he'd taken a billet of wood and smashed it in my face, and for a moment I couldn't see.

But then I stood up and went up to him, and he stepped out of the way as if he thought I'd do something to him, and I told him straight out:

"Someone ought to kill you. If this thing in my back hadn't happened. If I could use my arms. Then I'd kill you."

And he looked at me, he didn't say anything, there was nothing to argue about, he could see I meant what I said. So he took his fur coat and left, he even forgot to put down the almanac.

And after that it was a long time before he dared to come to us again.

In June of '74 Johanna had a boy. He was called Alexis after my mother's father.

My back got better. But it was as if my head had got stuck, I couldn't turn my neck. And my arms improved so I could lift my hands up to my shoulders, I could carve wooden things with a knife and I could mend shoes, and when the woodcocks started calling I could carry my gun again. But I wasn't a stacker any longer, I wasn't any use to them at Baggböle nor at any other sawmill. So I couldn't earn anything anymore.

But credit. We did have credit.

☐

Right from the beginning and on to the end.

That's how things were.

When Job was in despair, when he sat among the ashes and had rent his mantle, he asked:

"What is my strength, that I should hope? And what is mine end, that I should prolong my life? Is my strength the strength of stones? Or is my flesh of brass? Is not my help in me? And is wisdom driven quite from me?"

Finally I told Johanna that there was no mercy, we should try to help ourselves, for what did we have to lose? That too is a duty: to help oneself; what else could he take away from us?

Lord, what is the last mite?

She told me everything that used to happen when he claimed his dues, and it was as if she was cutting deep into me with a knife, but I knew I had to bear it, he always wanted it his own peculiar way, he was unnatural like that too, and it wasn't easy for Johanna to tell it all.

He'd said he'd come on Lady Day. I couldn't sleep that night.

When we heard his footsteps I went into the pantry and stood behind the door, I could see everything through the crack. Johanna sat down at the harmonium and I could see she was white in the face as if all her blood had run out.

But Karl Orsa didn't want music.

"Are the kids asleep?" he said. He looked his usual self, he looked like he did standing behind the counter in the shop.

And Johanna said what we'd agreed:

"They're asleep. They're asleep and Johnny has taken the gun and gone to Fir Hill."

I had a knife in my hand, and I thought, If only you

knew, Karl Orsa, that I'm standing here looking at you and that there's a knife in my hand . . .

"Eight crowns," he said to Johanna. "Eight crowns in the book."

And:

"No one can be burdened with debts for too long."

And:

"You're so pretty today. You blossom out more with every day that passes."

Then he went and lay down on the bed, and I thought Johanna looked like a sacrificial lamb, and I looked at the sheath knife, it was grandfather's. But it had also been Jacob's knife. And then he undid his trousers and made himself ready, and he looked his usual self, he looked the same as he did when he was displaying a piece of cloth or a hammer handle in the shop, and Johanna climbed up and sat on top of him.

And I only waited a moment, just long enough for the blood that dimmed my eyes to drain away, and then I threw open the door and ran over to them, and Johanna jumped out of the way just as we'd agreed, and I cut hard and fast like when you cut a chicken's throat, and Karl Orsa never had time to realize what was happening.

All I got in my hand was the last half inch of the head of his prick, it shrank like a snowball between my fingers.

I'd planned to tell him that from now on . . . But that just wasn't the way it went.

He sat up a little to see what I'd done, and Johanna stood behind me, a lot of blood was flowing and his prick wilted so there was almost nothing but skin left, and none of us said a word. I hadn't thought beyond that. I had no idea what would happen afterward.

But nothing much happened at all. It wasn't only his prick that wilted, it was as if we were all slack and empty. He'll bleed to death, I thought. Never before had I seen a person bleed so terribly from a single part of his body.

Johanna came to at last, and she took up her apron from the stool in front of the harmonium and folded it and bound up Karl Orsa to stop the blood from flowing, and her hands were as careful and gentle as if she were swaddling a baby, but she didn't say anything. And Karl Orsa said not a single word, he lay quite still and it looked as if this was what he'd been expecting.

That it must have been intended.

He lay there like that until it was dusk outside.

Then he got up and dressed, and his face was as white and expressionless as if he was asleep, and then he left.

And the only thing that was said when he'd gone was what Johanna said:

"What if he goes to Skellefteå? If he reports it?"

But I knew he'd never report it. How would he have explained it all?

That night, how I felt that night you alone know, Lord. It was like purgatory. I'd never before felt such guilt. And I thought, what if I'd killed him.

I don't know how Karl Orsa treated his wound. Whether he did it himself or had someone to help him. Maybe Tilda.

We didn't have credit anymore. Three small children and no income and only one milch cow and the hunting, I shot a stray reindeer at Ox Spring. You can't live more uncertainly than that. Only you, Lord, know how we managed.

At Midsummer Johanna earned five crowns from playing.

And one Sunday evening toward the end of summer, while I sat carving a cup for Alexis, Tilda came, Karl Orsa's Tilda, and she had only one message and she delivered it quickly, she didn't even come indoors:

"Father sent me," she said. "He said I should tell you that

if you need it and if you want to he's not unwilling. Regarding credit."

☐

In the end that was our only way out. Credit. His credit was our salvation. Though we never said it, that without the credit . . .

Credit is like a pitcher that goes often to the well.

At Epiphany in '76 Karl Orsa turned up again, he was his usual self, it was as if what I'd done with the knife had never happened. He'd been thinking about the music all over Christmas he said, he had half a sugarloaf for Sabina.

And Johanna played Christmas tunes for him.

And then he said:

"Perhaps we could settle up, Johanna."

And that's when I saw red again, if only I'd been prepared but I wasn't, he was as strange and unnatural as the way of a serpent upon a rock, and I clenched my fist as if I'd been holding the knife.

But in the end I pulled myself together so that I could say to him:

"My back's getting better with every day that passes. I'll soon be earning again."

"You won't be a man for several years yet, Johnny," he said. "And that's a fact."

Sabina was sitting on the bed with the sugarloaf, Johanna looked at her, her face was all shiny from the sugar, and Johanna said:

"I don't think I can bring myself to do it."

And then I said what I was sure would be the final word:

"You can't manage it any longer, Karl Orsa," I said. "Not after the treatment I gave you. You're like a cripple from now on as far as that's concerned."

"I've thought about it," said Karl Orsa. "And I think it'll be all right. It feels as if it wouldn't be impossible."

And then none of us knew what to say, there seemed no way out, we were naked before each other. And before you, Lord.

Finally Karl Orsa got up and put on his fur coat, and in the doorway he said:

"But you still play as beautifully as ever, Johanna."

He only said that because something had to be said, it wasn't really about the music, and Johanna never played as well as Mother or Eva did.

When he'd gone Johanna said:

"It's not because he wants to. It's only because of the debts."

"It's wickedness," I said. "Sheer wickedness."

And then she remembered a saying from the Bible:

"He that doeth evil hath not seen God."

"Are you trying to excuse him?" I said.

"No one can excuse him," she said. "But he's still a human being."

I've thought a lot about that since then, and even now I don't understand what she meant: "But he's still a human being."

I should have asked what it meant, but that just wasn't the way it went. The fact that you're a human being isn't an excuse for anybody. Yet it's as if it meant that we're not guilty of anything. As if human beings are never really responsible for anything. As if human beings had paid a bit of their debt right from birth just by taking on themselves the burden of living a human life.

Perhaps that was what she thought.

If you had to think like that about anyone, then it would be Karl Orsa.

But Johanna never settled up with him again. The last

debt we had in the shop was never paid off, and we no longer had any credit.

□

In March when he was at the market in Skellefteå Karl Orsa discovered that people usually paid a deposit when they occupied a croft, it might even be written in law, and down south they always did.

"A hundred and sixty crowns," he said when he came back. "And anyone who doesn't pay his deposit can be evicted. That's what the law says."

"That's more money than I've seen in my whole life," I said.

"It's a tidy sum," he said. "But there's nothing I can do about it. We're all subject to the law."

And he went on:

"You can't live the way you do, Johnny. A hand-to-mouth existence without order or method. It won't work in the long run."

"But what are you going to do with us?" said Johanna.

"I'm responsible for the place," he said. "That's the responsibility that's laid upon me."

And he also remembered a saying from the Bible: "As disorder and confusion lead to discord, so likewise doth order lead to peace."

"And Alexis?" said Johanna. "And Eva and Sabina? The little ones?"

"They aren't my children. Tilda's the only child I've got. I have the papers from the court. Tilda Markström. She's my only child."

"The children aren't guilty of any debts," said Johanna. "What would our Lord say about that kind of order?"

And he thought hard for a moment, and then he said something that was totally incomprehensible:

"Our Lord is order itself."

And after that there was nothing more that I or Johanna could say.

And the final thing he said was this:

"The deposit has to be paid before Midsummer. If not, you'll have to go. And the house."

Lord, the last mite doesn't exist. The last mite is the one that we can never pay.

□

Everything from the beginning to the end.

And that's what I wanted to ask you, Lord: Had you decided all this from the beginning? Were we all bound in the bundle of life with you? If that was so, who among us could be guilty of debt? And if then we had no guilt, why did you use us as if we were responsible for everything?

That's all I want to ask you about.

Was it really true, as Karl Orsa said, that you, Lord, are order itself?

When Job had lost all he had to lose, he said: "And after my skin worms destroy this body."

Are we to be pure and free from debt only then, and not before?

We woke up early on Midsummer's Day, it was really still night, we were woken up by a hellish din and racket up on the roof, there was such a banging and clattering and thudding that we thought the roof was about to cave in on us, and Johanna wanted to take the children and get down to the cellar.

But I realized straightaway what it was.

So I got up and put my clothes on and told Johanna just

to lie still and not to worry because I was going to deal with this, there was a frightful noise up on the roof but it would soon be quiet again, and I took the gun, the one that originally belonged to Jacob, and the shot and powder and fuses.

And then I went out and no one saw me, I went right around the house to the south side, and I got down behind the big rock that the children used to pretend was "home," and it was as if I thought, Now, at last!

It was Karl Orsa and two of his hands, they'd already broken off the guttering and lowest boards—it was Grandfather who'd laid that roof long ago so it was well made—and on top of the ridge beam stood Karl Orsa, he had a big ax in his hand and it looked as if he was wondering whether he should tackle the chimneystack or the roof ridge itself, he wasn't used to hard labor and exerting himself. And I stared up at him and tried to make sense of him, it was as if I felt a sort of need to understand his thoughts. We aren't responsible for our thoughts, they rise up in us like weeds whether we want them to or not, thoughts are like writing inside us, they can't be separated from the life you've given us to live, you've filled the mind of every man, Lord, with special kinds of thoughts.

And I believe Karl Orsa thought he had no choice. He had been set to live that life and to sow his talents. And that's what he was doing as he stood there on the ridge beam holding the big ax in his hand, he was trading with the talents that had been entrusted to him, he was free of debt and guilt, it was the same for him as it was for Paul: he did not that which he desired, but that which he abhorred.

That's how things were and to whom shall we go?

So I loaded the gun and primed the fuse and cocked the hammer and rested the barrel against the rock, and I felt no guilt. I took careful aim, I've always been a good shot, and I took my time because I didn't know whether to aim at his head or chest or stomach, a stomach wound can be worse than any other, so I moved the stock very slightly up and down and thought, Now, Karl Orsa! And then, right then, just as I was trying to make up my mind like that, you, Lord, created this incredible thing that lies before me and beneath my feet, you intervened at last, it was just as if Karl Orsa vanished from my sight, I couldn't see him anymore with my aiming eye, and when I moved my head to one side and opened both eyes I saw the whole lot, the house and the foundations and the chimneystack and the ground the house stood on and the columbine that Johanna had planted in front of the porch, the whole lot moving and sort of sliding down the hillside the house was built on, the lower part of the slope had separated or split away from the rest of the ground and was slipping down the hill. And there was a roar as if the whole hill was about to collapse, and a cloud rose above the edge where the house had vanished so you couldn't see a thing, and I thought it isn't true but perhaps Karl Orsa finally got too heavy for the earth to bear.

And Johanna! And the little 'uns who hadn't yet lived their lives!

And a saying from the Bible came into my mind: And he that sat on the cloud thrust in his sickle on the earth, and the earth was cleaved—and I took out the fuse and laid down the gun.

But then it eventually went quiet and the smoke cleared and the dust, and I stood up and went over to this edge, here where I'm sitting now, and my legs were shaking so much that I didn't think I'd make it, and there was a sort of film over my eyes. But there was nothing to see below the edge, just the sandy soil and gravel and scree, not so much as a piece of board or a nail and no sign of life, and I couldn't think at all, everything that my thoughts had clung to all those years was swallowed up and buried and not even the chimneystack was sticking up, and even today, to this very day, I don't know which of us it was that you, Lord, thought justice should be done to, your kingdom is the scepter of justice, whether it was me or Karl Orsa. Tilda seems to be his only heir.

Lord?

And though after my skin worms destroy this body, yet in my flesh shall I see God.